THE DeVil IN BLUE JEANS

STACEY KENNEDY

Also by Stacey Kennedy

Most Eligible Cowboy
Stranded with a Cowboy

Visit the Author Profile page
at Harlequin.com for more titles.

STACEY KENNEDY

Recycling programs
for this product may
not exist in your area.

ISBN-13: 978-1-335-04157-9

The Devil in Blue Jeans

Copyright © 2024 by Stacey Kennedy

Harlequin Enterprises ULC
22 Adelaide St. West, 41st Floor
Toronto, Ontario M5H 4E3, Canada
www.Harlequin.com

Printed in U.S.A.

For my devil in blue jeans...

J.T., our love story will always be my favorite.

Dear Reader,

The Devil in Blue Jeans explores emotional healing in the aftermath of infidelity, the death of a parent and a devastating car crash. Please always read with care.

Be gentle with yourself!

Stacey Kennedy

Prologue

"Charly, if you take another step up this mountain, I will shove you over the edge."

Halfway up the Absaroka Mountains, Charly Henwood glanced over her shoulder. Her best friend, Aubrey Hale's blue eyes glared in warning as she panted heavily, sweat dampening her shiny blond hair.

"We're not even at the top yet," Charly pointed out. "Just take a few breaths and we'll be done soon."

"I hate you," Aubrey groaned.

Charly fought her laughter as she glanced to the third member of their trio, Willow Quinn. She shifted the large backpack around her shoulders with her usual sweet smile in place and adjusted her messy side braid of strawberry blond hair, her twinkling green eyes gleamed subtly. "Oh, stop whining," Willow said to Aubrey. "It's not so bad."

"Liar," came the muttered reply from behind Charly.

Charly laughed as two backpackers walked by looking ready to call it quits.

Willow raised her arm in encouragement. "You're almost there," she shouted.

"That's another lie," Aubrey said, scoffing.

After the couple smiled and thanked Willow, she turned back to Aubrey and said, "That's not lying. That's cheering people on."

Aubrey grumbled something incoherent beneath her breath, and Charly just shook her head, chuckling to herself as they continued. Here were her two closest friends since kindergarten—Willow was like sunshine while Aubrey was always its shadow. They'd experienced it all together while growing up with their families in Ann Arbor, Michigan—joyful moments, sad moments and everything in between.

Five minutes later, Aubrey barked out a curse. "That's it. I'm done." She dropped her backpack to the ground and sank onto it. "I wanted to explore Rome, soak up some culture and history, but instead we ended up here in Montana, on this stupid mountain."

Charly took in the view, realizing they were close enough to where she needed to get them. She shrugged off her backpack, not really blaming Aubrey for her less-than-thrilled mood. Aubrey wasn't a hiker. The trip had been a graduation present to themselves before they started their adult lives and moved away from each other in hopes of catching their big dreams.

Aubrey pulled out her water bottle, taking a big drink

before speaking again. "So, we've hiked through forests, camped under the stars and seen erupting geysers and hot springs. Explain to me why this place beats Rome."

Charly smiled as she sat down on her backpack next to Aubrey, then pointed down at the valley below them. More importantly, the small town. "We're here for *that*." Timber Falls was north of Yellowstone National Park, along the Yellowstone River, with a population of a little over seven thousand. Nineteenth-century brick buildings lined the two-lane street, which housed art galleries, bookstores and boutiques that displayed an Old Wild West ambience amid homestyle eateries, with a stunning view of the mountain range at the end of the road.

She glanced to her friends. "Do you remember the pact we made when we were thirteen?"

Willow scanned the town below before scrunching her nose. "What are you talking about?"

"This," Charly said, pulling a piece of paper from her pocket. She unfolded it, revealing a drawing that was identical to the small town nestled in the valley they were overlooking. "When I was researching different wineries and breweries in search of the best booze on the market, I found this place." Timber Falls was known as a filming spot for many movies and brought in artists and writers in droves. Now Charly understood why. There was something magical about this place. Something far past beautiful. A pulsating energy that was as warm and welcoming as it was peaceful. "When I saw it, I almost fell out of my chair."

Aubrey accepted the paper, her gaze glued to the page. "The similarity is a bit eerie."

"Right?" Charly agreed. None of them were particularly talented artists, but the picture created the unmistakable impression of a Main Street with an Old West vibe and mountains at the end of it. They used to fantasize about staying together forever in this small town they'd created, just the three of them, and falling in love with rugged cowboys.

"You kept this drawing all this time?" Willow asked as Aubrey returned the paper to Charly.

Charly nodded. "I found it when I was packing." They all lived together in a small apartment in Berkeley while she and Willow attended the University of California together and Aubrey attended the Culinary Institute of America. But their lease was up, and their lives were about to change forever.

"Incredible," Aubrey said.

Charly agreed with a nod. "After I found it, I got to thinking. When we leave here, we're all going our separate ways." She looked to Willow. "You're off to Portland for your new fancy marketing job." Her gaze fell to Aubrey. "You're heading to Atlanta working beneath Chef Bisset. And I'm moving to Phoenix with Marcel to open the nightclub." She'd met Marcel in her freshman year in a philanthropy course. He'd swept her right off her feet, and even though it took another two years for them to get serious, she knew he was her one and only. "The world is our oyster now, but I don't want us to forget what we once dreamed of having together."

Aubrey tilted her head, and the flush of her cheeks faded away gradually. "What exactly are you proposing?"

Charly flashed them a smile. "I'm suggesting that we come up with a contingency plan—just in case the plans we have don't work out."

Willow scrunched her nose in confusion. "I still don't get it."

Charly gestured to the paper. "When I found the drawing, and then discovered this town so randomly, I figured it had to be a sign. So, that's why I brought us here." After they'd hiked out of Yellowstone Park, they had lunch in town. Sitting outside on the patio of a hundred-and-twenty-year-old restaurant, she loved everything Timber Falls had to offer with all its rustic heritage. They had spent the rest of the afternoon exploring the two-laned Main Street, before setting out on their final hike up the mountains. "I wanted to see if this town was as magical as I was hoping it'd be—"

"And it was," Willow interjected softly.

Charly nodded and glanced down at the town nestled at the base of the mountains. There was a hardware store and a movie theater that still had the old metal cinema marquee. The shops were eclectic and quaint, and the town had clearly been renovated to keep true to its old-town American roots. The people striding down Main Street weren't rushing to get anywhere. They were taking in the sunny, warm day, enjoying life, not letting it fly by.

From the sense of tight-knit community and friendly townsfolk every which way you looked, the place had all the things they had once thought was so different than their city life. And most importantly, real-life cowboys—just the type of man their young hearts once dreamed of. That was, before life got in the way and reality hit them that none of them were ever leaving the big city for small-town living.

Charly looked between her friends. "Let's make a pact— if by the time we turn twenty-eight, we aren't satisfied with life in our new cities, then we return to what we always dreamed of. We come back here and mesh our worlds together. We open a place of our own. I handle the bar." Glancing at Aubrey, she added, "You handle the restaurant." She met Willow's gaze. "You do the marketing."

Willow studied Charly for a few seconds before asking, "Why settle on twenty-eight?"

"That gives us two years to fix whatever has gone wrong in our lives before we turn thirty," Charly explained.

Aubrey laughed softly, shaking her head. "This is a silly deal. That's six years away. We'll be settled by then. Don't you think talking about this will jinx our future plans?"

Charly shrugged. "Maybe, but I'm just saying if our plans don't work out, let's go back to our pact. We took this trip as a last celebration before becoming adults and it all led us here. What do we have to lose?" She waved out to the town below that held so much heart. "If at twenty-eight we feel less content than now, let's move here and start over." Charly held out her hand. "Who's in?"

Willow smiled wide, placing her hand on top of Charly's. "I'm in!"

Aubrey rolled her eyes. "I don't know why either of you are so excited about this. You do realize making this pact is like wishing that our dreams fail?"

"No, Miss Uptight," Charly corrected. "We're making this pact so that we can protect our own happiness. We need to always look out for each other. And we deserve the happiness that our thirteen-year-old selves dreamed up."

Aubrey's eyes narrowed for a moment and then she smiled. "Okay, I'm in." She placed her hand atop Willow's. "Here's to having a plan B."

Charly grinned at Willow before they all lifted their hands, and Charly shouted, "To having a backup plan!"

One

Six years later…

Jaxon Reed clicked his tongue and the colt beneath him surged forward, its hooves pounding across the meadow of endless Montana beauty that had been in his family for generations. The wind brushed past his face as he narrowed his gaze at the sun beginning to dip in the sky. As he took a deep breath, the aroma of hot dirt and sweet berries wafted through the air. He eagerly filled his lungs, feeling an unmistakable sense of freedom that always accompanied long rides across the land.

Timber Falls Ranch was known for its top-notch quarter horses that were bought and shipped all throughout North America. Over one hundred horses on the ranch were raised in an old-fashioned way, remaining outdoors all year round and living off the land. The mares and their young occupied one field, while the geldings had their own space. Separately, in different fields, were the stallions. Many of those horses went on to be winners in rodeos, endurance trail rides and working hunter competitions.

Before he set out to check on the herd late in the afternoon, he had anticipated a quiet ride, but it soon became apparent that luck was not on his side today.

Out in the west, he found a chestnut mare lying on the grass, accompanied by her fellow herd members. Without hesitation, he clucked his tongue again and the colt beneath him leaped into a gallop across one of the valleys that lay between Yellowstone and Big Sky in Montana.

As Jaxon drew nearer to the mare, worry sank deep into his gut. The mare was lying on her side, breathing heavily and perspiring profusely. He pulled gently on his reins, speaking softly to the colt he had been training for the past month, who instantly responded to his words and slowed its pace.

In one swift movement, Jaxon swung his leg over the back of the saddle and tied up the reins around its horn. Assured that the colt wouldn't wander away, Jaxon pulled out a pair of gloves from the saddlebag before giving Casey, one of his farmhands, an urgent call.

When Casey answered, Jaxon said, "I'm sending you my location. Get the vet out here—we've got a mare in trouble."

"On it," Casey replied.

Jaxon sent his coordinates, tucked his phone away and slid his hands into the gloves before approaching the mare. "Easy, Mama," he murmured, striding around her. She had already birthed one of her foal's legs. Cursing, he got onto his knees behind her, steadying the foal with both feet during the next contraction before giving a strong pull.

Three contractions later, along with Jaxon's help, the baby horse slid out easily.

"Good. Good mama," he breathed, confirming the sweet bay filly wasn't in distress. Then he brought the foal closer to the mare's head and stepped away, giving them space, while the mare licked her baby.

Catching his breath, he returned to the colt, pulled off the gloves and threw them in his saddlebag for later disposal. "Well done," he told the colt before mounting him again.

Time ticked slowly as Jaxon watched the mare bond with her baby, when he heard the rumble of the ATV's engine before he spotted Casey driving up. The twenty-year-old had begun working on the ranch after graduating high school. Beside him sat Dr. Newman, the local vet who was well past retirement age.

After Casey cut the engine on the ATV, Dr. Newman jumped out, his deep brown eyes shining with excitement. "Your first foal since you took over the ranch."

Jaxon nodded in understanding. The thought hadn't been lost on him either. This was the first birth on the ranch since his father's untimely death from a heart attack six months ago. He shifted on his feet, the chilly awareness of the loss of his father clawing at his chest. The constant reminder was always there that he was still rocked to his core that his father was gone, and Jaxon had stepped into his father's very large boots at the ranch. "I got here just in time," he remarked, knowing had this happened overnight the mare likely would have died.

The doctor moved closer. "You've got the same knack as your father. He always seemed to know when it was time to come out here and check on his ladies."

Jaxon merely raised an eyebrow in response. His father did have a sixth sense when it came to horses, and he knew he had inherited it too. Becoming a third-generation breeder wasn't what he'd planned to do so suddenly, but he would never let his family's ranch break apart and lose its legacy.

He wasn't even sure if he'd had a chance to grieve his father's passing, or properly say goodbye to the life he had before he was weighed down with responsibility for the ranch. The moment his father died, Jaxon had dived into the business and never looked back.

The doctor started tending to the mare, and once Jaxon could see she was in good hands, he said to Casey, "I need to go check on the others in the herd. Give me a shout if you need me."

"Will do," Casey replied.

Jaxon gave a quick thank-you to Dr. Newman before giving another click of his tongue. The colt cantered away across the meadow full of wildflowers as they passed the wide spread of contented horses grazing on the grass and growing as they should.

As he and the horse ventured over a hill, Jaxon caught sight of the ranch with its breathtaking beauty and felt a warmth fill his chest, regardless that home looked unrecognizable without his father there. He'd grown used to a lack of female presence when his mother died from ovarian cancer when he was eight-years old, but his father's absence felt...*heavy*. With a sigh, he gently patted the colt's neck before settling into an easy walk, letting out some slack in the reins to allow the horse to cool off after their long ride.

Down the hill, a cozy three-bedroom house sat diagonally across from the barn. The pine logs and fieldstone structure had a rectangular sand ring in front for training, and a few large grassy paddocks for the horses. After his father's funeral at the ranch that brought in hundreds of horsemen to say their final goodbyes to a man they respected, Jaxon moved from his cabin on the northern part of the land and into the house that his father had built.

As Jaxon arrived at the barn, Gunner Woods walked across one of the fields toward him, wearing tan-colored chaps over his blue jeans. A black cowboy hat was perched atop his stylish blond hair and his bright blue eyes glinted with amusement.

Gunner had lived in Nashville for a short time, pursuing his music career. When he'd come back to town after his album failed to deliver, Jaxon had hired him as a trainer without much thought and Gunner had moved into Jaxon's cabin. Their shared high school memories forged a bond between them that could not be broken, and Gunner's soft approach with young horses had always impressed Jaxon.

"Everything okay?" Gunner asked when he reached him.

"The mare and foal are fine. Doc is with them now." Jaxon dismounted his colt and strode halfway to Gunner. "This guy is ready to be sold."

"Good news all around," Gunner said, propping himself up against the fence post.

"Done with him?" Wayne called, coming out of the barn. The gangly eighteen-year-old had gotten his start at the farm like any other kid. He'd stacked hay bales, cleaned the stalls and groomed the horses.

Jaxon let go of the reins. "That's it for today," he answered. "We've got somewhere else to be now." If only Wayne was old enough to come along too.

"Where's that?" Wayne asked, taking the horse's reins over his head.

Jaxon shot Gunner a grin. "We've got a date with some cold beers."

"Ah," Gunner said with sudden realization. "The bar reopened today, didn't it? I completely forgot."

Jaxon couldn't forget. Before his father's death, Jaxon had owned a bar on Main Street. He'd opened the bar in the evenings and pitched in at the ranch during the day for a few hours. But after his father died, Jaxon had known he had to devote himself exclusively to ensuring their family business survived, so he'd sold the bar.

He was proud of what he'd brought to the town—a place where the locals felt like they belonged. It had been seven weeks since the town had a legitimate bar as opposed to just restaurants that served alcohol, and Jaxon could practically taste the crisp craft lager on his tongue.

He was also itching for a fun night out, something he hadn't had in months besides a campfire and beers at the ranch. Word in town was all the twenty-somethings had been complaining about Jaxon's bar shutting down, considering the closest bar catering to the younger crowd was an hour away in a larger city. He was not the only one looking for a new hot spot to cut loose. "I have never been so ready for a damn beer," he commented.

Wayne mumbled something inarticulate about being young and wished them a good time as he led the horse away.

Jaxon chuckled, hearing tire treads crunching against gravel behind him. He looked over his shoulder right as Eli Cole pulled up in a truck with a horse trailer attached to it.

His childhood friend had moved away to Seattle, where he'd owned a carpentry business before settling back home after his sister had passed away. Jaxon and Gunner had never experienced having siblings but found family in each other over the years, and Eli had been there right next to them.

Eli eventually parked the truck and trailer next to Jaxon's vehicle and got out. His dark hair poked out from beneath his worn cowboy hat while his wise green eyes glimmered from underneath. "Delivery went smoothly," he remarked in his gravelly voice.

The latest delivery was a five-year-old filly Eli had trained himself. Their three-man team operated flawlessly, as they'd all grown up on this ranch, working their summers and weekends under the guidance of Jaxon's father.

"Up for a beer?" Jaxon asked Eli.

"Been waiting on this all day," Eli replied with a smirk. "Let's get out of here."

Jaxon was sure that luck was finally on his side today.

Until he arrived at the rustic town square of Timber Falls twenty minutes later, and his mood took a nosedive.

The Old West vibe of the bar's storefront was gone, replaced by sleek black modern windows. After selling the bar seven weeks ago—choosing to know nothing about the buyers aside from their promise to keep the place a bar, so the town wouldn't lose its hot-spot—he hadn't come to town. The renovation would have ripped his heart out. The only consolation was knowing that the space he created that gave the hardworking people of Timber Falls a place to unwind and enjoy would continue.

But as he opened the bar's door, which now opened easily and didn't need a little force as it used to, he walked straight into hell.

The walls were no longer adorned with license plates. Now they were painted light gray and the wood paneling on the lower half was stained white. The moose head trophy from a hunting trip with his father and grandfather now wore a pink feather boa and sparkly sunglasses, while the tables and bar stools remained unchanged. In place of the mirror on the back wall hung a banner proclaiming She overcame everything that was meant to destroy her. The greasy aroma normally emanating from bar food had been replaced by an unexpected floral scent.

Jaxon removed his cowboy hat as he took a seat at one of the booths. The blaring country music had been replaced by a Taylor Swift song, and freshly cut flowers had taken the place of a bowl of peanuts. Two women stood behind the bar wearing pink shirts with THE NAKED MOOSE scrawled across them.

"This is something," Eli muttered, sliding into the booth across from Jaxon.

"That's one way to put it," Gunner said, adjusting the waistline of his Levi's before sitting next to Eli.

"Hmm," Jaxon agreed.

A cute ginger-haired woman came up to greet them. Her name tag read Willow. "Welcome to The Naked Moose's grand opening. What can I get you?"

She talked like a city girl, sounding from the Midwest. Obviously, the bar's new owners weren't from around here.

"A beer," Jaxon replied.

Her cheeks flushed bright pink as she handed him a menu featuring only cocktails. He gave the menu back. "A Budweiser please." A store-bought beer was better than nothing.

Willow shook her head apologetically, letting out a soft "um."

The other woman standing at the bar hurried to Willow's side. Her name tag read Aubrey.

Before Jaxon even looked over at Gunner, he knew his

friend would be grinning at this woman. He always did have a thing for blondes, and she was just his type.

Aubrey smiled tightly and presented him a plate of small rainbow-colored cookies. "Macaron?"

Jaxon shook his head and gestured at the bar. "Plain old beer, if you don't mind." Everyone in town had anticipated the reopening of this place—especially after Jaxon had abruptly shut it down—but *this*…what the hell was this?

His real estate agent, Billy Palmer, told him the bar would be restored and revived by its new owners. Not…turned into a big-city cocktail lounge, where the hardworking townsfolk would feel not only out of place but unwelcome. He and his friends were coated in layers of dust. Their hands were grimy, their faces caked in the stuff. His gaze drifted to where they'd walked in and left a path of dirt along the spotless floors. Every damn spot in this bar sparkled. He felt like he'd stepped into a place that not only didn't cater to anyone he knew in Timber Falls, the people he respected and valued, but that did not belong in a small rustic town.

He'd built his bar with only one thought in mind: provide a fun space that got to the heart of what the town and the people needed. A place where there was always dirt on the floors for the cowboys who came, a place where sports were playing on the television screens to appease fans, music and dancing for the people looking to party, and the best craft beer out there. Nothing in this space resembled the bar he'd dreamed up, and his heart twisted in agony over watching his dream burn.

"Can I help you?"

Jaxon's gaze jerked toward the sound of a firm yet sul-try voice. The woman standing before him had flames in her light brown eyes, a color that reminded him of cognac. Her long brunette curls were twisted around her oval face, and all his focus went straight to her full lips, now pressed together in annoyance.

"That depends," he replied, glancing at her name tag that read Charly. He uttered her name, liking how it rolled off his tongue.

She gave him a bored stare. "On?"

"Got any beers here?"

Her expression was stern. "Sorry, we don't carry beer. We're a cocktail lounge."

Jaxon held her intense stare, enjoying the challenge in the depths of her eyes. Oddly, he felt drawn into it, even if she had something to do with the fact that the bar he had cherished no longer had any of the elements that made it the town's hotspot.

He tore his gaze away and noticed a chalkboard that pro-claimed Book your divorce party today!

"I'll have scotch on the rocks," he said, finally glancing her way again. Eli and Gunner ordered the same.

"Coming right up," Charly said before walking away, revealing her ripped shorts that Jaxon shouldn't be ogling.

And yet...*and yet*...he couldn't look away.

After she returned and handed them their drinks, she

gave a polite smile. "Thanks for coming to the grand opening. Enjoy your drinks."

Life in Timber Falls was always the same. Every day just like the last. But *that* woman was not like anyone he'd ever met before. "I'll see you again soon, Charly," he promised, calling after her.

She glanced back and grinned, all teeth. "Let's not make it too soon."

He smiled after her. He'd never been shut down so fast. *Oh, hell, who is this woman?*

"You weren't expecting this, were you?" Eli asked when she was out of hearing distance.

Jaxon raised an eyebrow at him. "The state of my bar or the woman who looks like she wants to stab me in the eye?"

Gunner laughed.

"Both," Eli said, his mouth twitching.

"Both are surprising," Jaxon admitted. "But one is more unwelcome than the other." Taking a sip of his scotch, Jaxon found that at least they had chosen top-shelf alcohol.

Gunner knocked back his glass in one go and then asked, "What are you going to do?"

Jaxon just shrugged. "What can I do? They own the bar now." He never expected that whoever took over his bar would change it so drastically. The bar looked plucked out of New York City. The residents of Timber Falls lived there for its rustic roots, not modern luxuries.

While Jaxon had catered his bar to the needs of everyone in town, the hardworking ranchers held a special place there. He'd grown up around the men and women who worked the land and cattle for generations. His father had close ties to every rancher in the area, and Jaxon had seen they had lacked a place to get together and enjoy some beers and laughs.

His bar meant something to the people of Timber Falls. It meant something to him. And these big-city ladies seemed determined to make sure the favorite weekend spot and after-work hangout was transformed into a place where the only people who would feel welcome there were out-of-towners.

With a thick taste of disappointment in his mouth, he scowled at the glitter and feathers. "What could be their motive?" he questioned. "They're pretty much alienating all their beer-drinking customers."

Eli said, "Big cities have cocktail lounges."

"This isn't a big city," Gunner said.

He felt an ache in his chest as he considered what they'd done to his bar. "This won't stand," he said eventually. "For years, this bar belonged the people of Timber Falls who want a rugged experience that included great beer, not...*this*." He scraped a hand across the scruff on his face. "I need to fix this."

Eli had his glass halfway to his mouth. "How do you plan on doing that?" he asked.

Jaxon glanced at Charly talking with another customer he didn't recognize—a tourist he'd bet—and took a sip of his scotch. He savored the flavor of the oak barrels it was aged in before answering, "We need to show them what this bar means to Timber Falls."

Gunner snorted. "And you think you're going to be the one to show her that?"

"Who better is there?" Jaxon challenged confidently.

Eli burst out laughing and shook his head in disbelief as he gestured toward Charly. "Anyone, Jaxon. Absolutely anyone would be better than you. She looked ready to cut you."

Not deterred, Jaxon threw back the remainder of his drink. His gaze followed Charly's movements as she headed to the other end of the bar. As if aware he was speaking about her, she turned her head and their eyes met. Hers narrowed.

An amused grin spread across his face. "She isn't so bad. Even if those claws are sharp."

"Sharp?" Eli snorted. "I'd say they're downright deadly."

Gunner agreed with a nod and asked, "What will happen if you fail to convince her to bring beer back?"

"I won't fail," Jaxon declared with conviction. He winked at his friends and leaned across the table to add, "You know I'm always up for a challenge, especially one that's a pretty brunette."

Two

The following morning, Charly was cozied up on a small patio out front of the breakfast hot spot Sparrow Catching. Her nose crinkled at the exhaust from an old Ford truck driving along Main Street. She gazed out at the two-laned road, reminded how different this small town was compared to the bustling city. The towering skyscrapers and honking taxis were replaced with friendly neighbors waving to one another, cowboy hats adorning most heads and barely a single high heel in sight. The nightlife was nonexistent. Nevertheless, it was easy for her to fall in love with the rustic town square, just like she had all those years ago.

The buildings were a blend of stained wood and stone, with towering mountains at the end of the road. Scattered among the stores was an ice cream parlor, a coffeehouse and a sweets shop. Every Saturday, part of the road was blocked off to make way for the bustling farmers market.

In comparison to her former life in Michigan and, more recently, Arizona, Charly was still adjusting to all the differences in small-town life. Over the last seven weeks, since they'd all packed up their lives and moved to Timber Falls, she'd stopped missing the rowdiness of the bar she'd left behind in Phoenix and the hustle and bustle of the city. In Timber Falls, life seemed to move at a different pace. People here appeared to appreciate one another in a way that she had never seen anywhere else.

But she still couldn't help but feel her entire life was back in Phoenix. Not that long ago, her life had been all planned out. Until Marcel, the man Charly once planned to marry and had owned a successful bar with in Phoenix, broke her heart by cheating on her with their head bartender, Hannah, destroying any future plans for the two of them.

Even now, as she sat there, she knew she was still finding her footing in Timber Falls, trying to build a life that was better than the one she'd had with Marcel, but even she knew Timber Falls didn't really feel like it belonged to her yet.

She shook away the thought, no use getting hung up on it. The only way forward now was not looking back into the past and the heartbreak that lay there.

Glancing across the table, she knew she wasn't the only one adjusting. Willow and Aubrey had gone through hard times over the past few years too. Willow had endured an abusive ex-boyfriend. Aubrey had quit her job in Atlanta because of harassment from her boss.

Now they'd called in their pact and were all starting over, trying to fix all the things that had gone so very wrong in their lives.

A *clang* drew her gaze to the owner of the diner, Jenna. With her curly brown hair bouncing on her shoulders, she arrived at their round table, where they sat in metal chairs decorated with flower-patterned cushions.

Aubrey said with eagerness, "Seriously, Jenna, these waffles are the best I've ever had."

Willow gave a light smile. "She's beyond picky about food, so you can trust what she said."

Aubrey rolled her eyes at Willow before suggesting to Jenna, "Have you thought about having weekly waffle dessert specials?"

Jenna gave a questioning tilt of her head. "What do you mean?"

"What if you had different flavors every week?" Aubrey offered. "Like a cinnamon bun waffle one week, then s'mores the next or maybe hazelnut banana crunch. You could bring in lots of people that way—teenagers, date nighters, everyone."

"That's a brilliant idea," Jenna said, topping up Charly's coffee. "I hadn't considered that before."

Aubrey beamed.

"It's her specialty—she's a brilliant chef," Charly said with a laugh, but she meant it—Aubrey had come up with amazing recipes ever since she was a child. Being a chef seemed ingrained into her DNA.

Jenna finished topping off Aubrey's coffee. "Well, if you have any other ideas, send them my way, all right?"

"You got it," Aubrey said with a proud nod.

As Jenna walked away, Charly stirred some sugar into her coffee and remarked, "They could do a lot with this place."

Aubrey nodded in agreement. "The whole town needs an update if it wants to stay relevant."

Charly gazed around at the space, which had an energy to it that was both inviting and tranquil, as Willow said, "I don't know. Modern isn't always good. To take away all the Old West vibe will steal away the charm."

"Maybe." Aubrey shrugged. "But keeping up with the times isn't a bad thing either."

Charly agreed with a nod. Aubrey always encouraged them to reach higher and strive for more, while Willow supported them through every phase of their lives. As for Charley, she thought of herself as the planner who added excitement into the mix.

"Willow, my dear!"

Willow lit up as Betty—an eighty-year-old widow with tight, purplish-gray curls—approached her with a beaming smile. "Hi, Betty, how are you?" She rose to give Betty a warm embrace.

"I'm well, sweetheart," Betty replied before presenting Willow with a stack of hand-knit dishcloths. "I made these for you."

"Thank you so much," said Willow enthusiastically. "You know I love these."

Although Charly enjoyed them too, they had a whole drawer full of knitted dishcloths already, but Charly would never say a word to Willow about it as she watched her accept them appreciatively. After all, Charly relied on Willow's kind heart during her darker moments.

After Betty left, they finished their coffee and, the bill settled, lingered to talk with everyone in the restaurant. Charly knew that mingling with the locals was crucial to being accepted in this town. Breakfast at the diner each morning quickly became a strategy to fit in, but it also turned into something they had all come to look forward to.

The townsfolk in Timber Falls were amazing people— until the grand opening yesterday. Now, and even this morning, they'd received more than a few nasty looks. No one seemed thrilled that they'd modified the Western bar into a chic cocktail lounge.

Opening an upscale bar in this small town had seemed like an excellent idea, since the town lacked modern luxuries. And because Charly and her friends were mending broken hearts, they wanted to create a place where women could come together and heal from their pain. They wanted a place that brought women together and celebrated them, while also providing the town with something it lacked, a higher-end bar.

Only, she hadn't anticipated the regulars who frequented the bar would feel annoyed over their plans.

Charly pushed memories of yesterday aside as she and her best friends left the restaurant, walked down Main Street and arrived at the bar to begin their usual routine as a couple customers started to file in.

Willow and Aubrey got right to work, serving the customers, but Charly hung back, silently watching. *This bar must succeed. Failure is not an option.* Her last bar with Marcel had ended up never feeling like hers, since he made all the decisions. She needed this bar to succeed not only financially for Willow and Aubrey too, but to prove to herself she didn't need Marcel for success. And she needed something to feel good about. Because right now, she had a hard time looking at herself in the mirror after Marcel's betrayal.

Shaking off the worry seeping into her bones, she got to work.

It wasn't until after the lunch rush that the worry hit her again straight in the chest.

"Well, that was a total disappointment," Aubrey said after the last customers left.

Charly nodded as she closed the ice bucket. "The afternoon rush was no rush at all." They'd had a total of ten customers, and Charly got the feeling none of them were locals. Opening day had gone so well. The bar had been packed...even if most of the people looked miserable. "I don't know what happened."

Willow gathered the empty glasses on the bar. "It's only our second day. I bet things will pick up."

Charly agreed with a nod, but the concern tickling in her throat reminded her that this bar could not fail. Not only for her pride, but because then they would all have to admit that their lives had gone to total shit. Needing space, she headed toward the back and called out, "I'll be in my office if anyone needs anything."

She left Willow and Aubrey chatting about marketing ideas and retreated to her office to focus on emails and sorting out the books to look for any wiggle room in case things were slower than she anticipated going into this.

It was 6:10 p.m. when she left the back room of the bar once again, expecting the dinner crowd and post-work rush to soon follow. She resurfaced from the back only to find the bar too quiet. Her eyes immediately darted to a particular booth; it was the same as yesterday, filled with those two cowboys...and that one devil.

"There must be something in the water around here," Aubrey muttered, sidling up to Charly. "These cowboys are seriously hot."

Every cowboy in that booth wore the same miserable expression. "And they know it too," Charly replied, wiping a small spill off the counter. She looked up to see two women at the end of the bar, their heads bent over their phones and laughter spilling from them, before she returned her attention to her friends. "Focus, girls. We need to ensure this place turns a profit, not get distracted by cowboys, no matter how handsome they may be."

Aubrey gave her a pointed look and sly grin. "Ha! So you admit you weren't immune to that guy over there?"

Charly began rinsing out the cloth in silence, refusing to further indulge that conversation. She hated admitting she had been taken in by the cowboy's silver-blue eyes and mischievous smile. He had stood around six-two with an impressive build beneath his gray T-shirt and worn jeans from all those days on the ranch. His light brown hair was well-kept, ending with a neatly trimmed beard. Once upon a time she would've melted at his feet, but love wasn't her priority anymore.

Willow came to lean against the bar, resting her chin on one hand as she said, "I don't think anyone can resist their appeal. Just look at them—they're gorgeous!"

Charly wrung out the moist cloth and hung it up to air-dry on the faucet. "Girls, we all know why we're here. We've been through a lot lately, but now it's time for us to have something that's only ours and to make something new of ourselves. This is our chance to start fresh." She looked between her friends. "Have you forgotten that we are all starting over? That this is our dream, and it won't come true unless we make it happen? Men broke our dreams. They cannot be our priority now."

Aubrey rested upon the ice bucket, folding her arms over the newly printed black T-shirt with THE NAKED MOOSE written in a calligraphy font across the chest. "No, I haven't forgotten that I'm twenty-eight and my life has pretty much crumbled around me."

Willow huffed out a laugh. "As if I'd forget," she said.

Charly's throat tightened, and she gently placed her hand on Willow's arm in comfort. "Let's stay focused," she reminded them. This bar was their new beginning and they only had one chance at success—no man was going to take that away from them. "We need to do whatever we can to get ahead."

Willow smacked the countertop with her palm. "Agreed."

Aubrey nodded, then glanced over her shoulder at the cowboys in the booth. "Though I may be tempted to admire them from afar," she added with a playful smile.

"Look, not touch," Charly said firmly, before approaching the women at the end of the bar. "Are you doing okay, ladies?"

"We're doing just fine." The pair exchanged meaningful looks before the blonde quietly said, "I'm Becky and this is Hilary."

Charly smiled. "Nice to meet you. I'm Charly. Behind me are Willow and Aubrey."

Her friends waved from afar as Becky said, "I have a piece of advice for you all. We saw you looking at that group of cowboys over in that booth, and woman to woman, stay away from that one over there with the beard. Jaxon Reed is pure trouble. He'll make you a notch on his bedpost and that's it."

Jaxon… Not a bad name, Charly thought to herself.

Willow stepped closer to the women, all eagerness for some juicy gossip. "What do you know that we don't?"

Becky said quietly, keeping the conversation private, "He's a heartbreaker. Really, you should stay clear of all of them from Timber Falls Ranch. They like being lone wolves."

A mischievous glint appeared in Willow's eyes as she prodded Charly aside to get closer to the women. "Why?"

Hilary leaned in, keeping their conversation quiet. "They're all running away from something. Believe me, they don't bring anything but heartache." She paused to shrug. "If you're looking for a fun time, sure, go for it. But don't give them your hearts—they'll only crush them."

Charly readjusted the tubs of limes and lemons beneath the counter. "We're not looking for fun, or anything else." She had a chance to make this bar a success without relying on a man, like she had with Marcel. With their bar, she'd let his ideas overpower hers. She'd overlooked all his red flags and somehow let herself believe he loved her, even accepting his proposal. Now she knew better. Men didn't change. Red flags lasted forever. "I appreciate your warning. Thanks for the heads-up, but none of us are looking for love."

Becky snorted with amusement. "But you're in Timber Falls—love finds you here. You'd better watch out."

Hilary nodded in agreement. "Didn't you know? There's an old legend about this place and magic in the Absaroka Mountains. The locals say that it's the perfect recipe for love—the clean air, the energy in the mountains, and all the blue skies and water. Anyone who moves into town will find their soulmate."

Willow leaned forward eagerly. "For real?"

"It's an old story that locals tell," Hilary started explaining, twirling her martini glass around with her fingers.

Charly replied quickly, her tone implying finality, "That won't include me."

Becky grinned while Hilary flashed their matching wedding rings as evidence of the "legend" and its power. "That's what they all say," said Hilary with a mischievous glint in her eyes. "But we were once like you too."

Charly still felt the weight missing from her finger where her engagement ring used to be. She had wanted love. Ever since she was a kid with boy band posters on her wall, she'd dreamed of finding her one true love. But that dream had burned up when she'd caught Marcel with another woman. The life she'd thought she'd live with him had died that day, and now she was scrambling to build a new dream for herself.

A lump caught in her throat, and she cleared it away with a cough. "Anything else you need?" she asked, looking up at Becky and Hilary.

"I'll have another round," Becky replied, holding up an empty glass.

Hilary nodded in agreement. "Me too."

"Coming right up." Charly collected the glasses and moved down to the long mirror on the wall that stretched along the shelves filled with bottles of alcohol. At the same time, Aubrey was just coming back from delivering snacks to the cowboy booth. She said, "Look how polite they are—they all took off their hats when they sat down to eat."

Charly hadn't realized it, but she saw now that each cowboy's hat was neatly lined up on the windowsill next to the booths. In the city, men often wore baseball caps in bars without taking them off.

She didn't want to lose their vision about turning the

bar into a space to celebrate female achievements and help women mend broken hearts, but she didn't want to alienate the cowboys and the regulars who obviously had loved this place before too. "Maybe we should install some hooks or something for them to hang their hats on," Charly suggested, thinking out loud.

Aubrey nodded. "That would be useful."

Willow sidled up to them and said, "So, for our first ladies' night tomorrow, I have a feeling we need something extra special to get people talking. But at this point, I don't have any ideas beyond what we've already planned. Did either of you think of something? Anything that could really make an impression?"

Charly had already been considering this. She started to mix vodka and cranberry juice into two martini glasses for cosmopolitans. "I don't have anything yet, but it might come to me later," she said. "I'll keep thinking about it." She hated how slowly ideas were coming to her. Before she'd been cheated on, she was sharp and trusted her intuition. Now her judgement felt shaken.

"Same here," Willow said as she checked her watch. "I'm going to do some research online too. Maybe I'll find something there."

"I need to make some apps," Aubrey said, following behind and heading toward the kitchen.

As Charly grabbed the triple sec, she was busy pondering ways to draw in ladies from all around the area. They needed something incredible, something that would get talked about throughout town.

"Charly."

She felt the weight of Jaxon's gaze before turning around to greet his familiar grin—the same one she'd seen many times on Marcel's face. That grin only belonged to a man full of confidence. She used to love a smile like this. Now she frowned at it. "Need another drink?" she asked.

He shook his head. "We're just about to head out. But I got to thinking—how about I show you around Timber Falls and take you to all the good spots?" He settled onto a stool, planting his elbows on the bar top.

She restrained her scoff. He didn't even bother to get to know her before trying to make his move. Becky and Hilary were right—this guy thought he was at the top of his game. "Do you always ask out women you just met?"

"Nope." His answer was fast and decisive.

Putting her back to him, she poured triple sec into a martini glass. "Thanks for the offer, but I don't do that anymore."

"Do what?"

"Date."

"Ever?"

"Never again." She put the bottle back on its shelf and added an orange peel twist to the glasses before taking them to the two ladies. Becky gave her a warning glance when she handed it over, but Charly didn't comment.

Returning to Jaxon, she replied, "Do you want to settle up your bill?"

Jaxon fixed her with a steady look. "Why don't you date?"

"It's exhausting," she said simply.

Amusement glinted in his eyes as he asked, "What about drinks between friends, then?"

"We're not friends," she pointed out firmly.

He smiled his dazzling smile again. "Not yet we're not. But we could be if you let me."

Charly took a deep breath, examining him. Certainly, she had a few options here. She could shut him down with one sharp remark or end it in the most courteous way possible, but an idea suddenly began to form—one that would rival any scheme a player could come up with. "All right, let's meet for drinks here tomorrow evening at eight o'clock. Bring your buddies too!"

"Drinks it is," he said with a devastating smile that likely charmed many women. Even Charly felt an urge to get a little closer to him. "See you then."

She quickly turned away before she changed her mind about her decision.

"Hey, Charly," he called after her, and when she glanced back over her shoulder, he winked and said, "Get some good rest tonight. I don't want you tired for our...drinks."

Charly returned the grin and replied teasingly, "Please, cowboy, you won't be able to keep up."

His low, throaty chuckle was full of things that made her

body heat and remained with her the entire night she kept busy serving customers   yet more concerning was how she laughed along with him. It dawned on Charly then just how long it had been since she had laughed so carefreely. Too long.

By the time she pulled up in front of the light blue house on Quiet Oak Road that she'd bought with Willow and Aubrey later that night after they closed the bar, Charly did, in fact, feel exhausted. The day had been long and tiresome. Hell, the last seven weeks had been draining.

As she parked in their driveway, her cell phone burst into life. One glance at the screen had her heart leaping into her throat. Only Marcel would call at two o'clock in the morning. He was probably drunk. She stepped out of the car and answered the call. "I hope you rot in a bucket of your own vomit," she said to Marcel before abruptly hanging up.

Willow chuckled, shutting the car's door behind her. "I see that jerk is still trying to call."

Charly followed Aubrey and Willow through a white gate leading to a cobbled path and up to the dark oak entrance door. Their house was straight out of a Western movie with flowered wallpaper, a grand foyer with an elegant wooden staircase and large windows allowing plenty of natural light during the day. From their backyard they could spot mountains off in the distance, while wildflowers scattered throughout the green space meant there was always fresh cut blossoms on their kitchen table. Huge trees framed the quarter-acre property, which attracted birds and other wildlife.

The real estate prices in Timber Falls were much cheaper than in the larger cities. Using the money they got from selling their homes, all three shared the expense and owned the house debt-free, except for the bar. That they held a mortgage on, which gave them even more reason to make it a success.

Once Willow opened the front door, Charly told her, "Marcel thinks we should talk things over. I legit don't get what he wants to talk about?" She'd walked in on him screwing the head bartender right on the bar. What could he possibly say?

She hadn't talked to him since that day. She got on an airplane that night and headed to Aubrey, then hired a company to pack up her belongings. She'd only been in Atlanta two weeks before they'd FaceTimed Willow and all decided that fate had led them to the pact.

Everything after that had happened so fast. They bought the bar in Timber Falls and then the house, and the rest was history.

Aubrey shut the front door behind her and scoffed. "You don't owe Marcel anything, not even a moment of your time."

Willow proceeded to the kitchen and Charly took up residence on the comfy living room couch full of mismatched throw pillows, rubbing her sore feet.

Aubrey joined her. "I really hope the bar gets busier."

"You and me both." Charly nodded in agreement, switching to the other foot. "Tomorrow is what will either make or break us."

Tomorrow was their first big event to celebrate women, and they needed the ladies in town and out to talk about it.

"I agree," said Willow as she returned with a tray of hummus and crackers and cheese. She placed it on the coffee table. "One idea I had was playing Smash or Pass and having hot actors printed on posters."

"That sounds fun," Aubrey commented.

Charly nodded in approval. "I like that too, but we also need to talk about those peeved regulars who keep coming in. We have seriously pissed some people off."

"No kidding," Willow said, as she put some cheese on a cracker. "We don't want people to hate us before we even get going."

"Maybe we just need to show them we're part of their inner circle, so to speak," Charly said. "What if we got Jaxon, the cowboy those ladies were talking about, to take part in a date auction?"

Willow's eyebrows shot up. "What could possibly make him agree to that? He doesn't know us."

Aubrey popped a piece of cheese into her mouth before saying, "Let's hear it."

Charly dunked a cracker into the hummus and said before she ate it, "Point one—Beck and Hilary said he loves women. He'll be sure to accept a bit of attention. Point two—if we want the town talking, why not auction off the guy every woman wants and use the proceeds for charity?"

Willow hesitated, munching her cracker. "It would certainly get tongues wagging. And helping the community is always a good thing. But which charity should we choose?"

Charly grabbed her cell phone and showed them the website she had found earlier. As soon as Willow saw the screen said Haley's Place, her eyes welled. It was a shelter for women who had been abused.

Handing the phone to Aubrey, Willow gave a sad smile. "This is just right for us. Thank you for finding it."

"I think it's perfect," Aubrey concurred.

Charly smiled, knowing this was good for Willow too. Helping others who faced what she had could only benefit her.

"While I love this idea," Aubrey said, "I'm not sure this cowboy will say yes, even if it is for charity. We don't even know him."

Charly glanced between her friends and grinned. "Don't worry. I'll take care of the cowboy." She paused to shrug. "Besides, he can always say no and back out if he doesn't want to, and I'll have a backup plan in case that happens. But something tells me he'll love being center stage."

Willow laughed and shook her head in disbelief. "I'd usually doubt you here, but I've seen your persuasive skills in action. You'll get him to agree one way or another."

Charly tossed the last cracker into her mouth and grinned confidently. "You got that right."

Three

The next morning, Jaxon delivered two horses to their new owners and then took some time to train the three colts he'd taken under his wing. Around midday, he had started receiving phone calls from loyal regulars at the bar, angry at him for selling the place to big-city outsiders who didn't understand life in Timber Falls.

By late afternoon, he was exhausted and needed a pick-me-up when he finally reached Main Street and parked his truck at the curb. He left the vehicle and walked into The Book Bean café, where he was greeted with the aroma of coffee, dusty paper and spices as the door chimed.

On one side were shelves of books and round tables filled with bestsellers on display. On the other side customers sat in comfortable chairs with their drinks. Meanwhile, Jaxon could hear pages being turned crisply and the espresso machine brewing up a strong roast.

Behind the counter stood Isabella, a pregnant brunette with a kind smile. "Jaxon," she said warmly. "Good to see you."

"Same to you," he answered, as he stopped at the counter, where the tip jar was half filled. He had dated Isabella back in high school. It hadn't lasted long after he'd kissed another girl at the school dance and Isabella, rightly so, had dropped him on his ass. "So how are things?"

Isabella lightly patted her round belly and said, "The little guy is a week late now, and I want him out."

"Too comfy in there, huh?" he asked as he reached into his back pocket for his wallet.

"Apparently so," she said as she went to get his usual coffee. When she set the paper cup down in front of him, she added, "I'm starting to feel like this is going to be an eternity of pregnancy."

He chuckled and took out a five-dollar bill before putting it on the counter. "Let's hope not for your sake. Take care of yourself."

"Thanks," she replied and tried to give him change but he had already started walking away.

He always gave tips to small businesses since he knew firsthand how difficult it was to get them established. When he'd owned the bar, it had been successful because he'd used all the money he'd earned during summers working for his father. But Isabella had started from scratch by renting the place first before buying it out. Even if he would never say it out loud, that extra tip every day was also, in a small way, an apology for how he'd treated her in high school.

As he continued down the street, passing old trucks and friendly faces, he waved and greeted everyone while two women near the sidewalk smiled at him warmly.

Jaxon walked on and entered the next door on his left, finding Billy's assistant, Sara, sitting behind her desk.

"Hey," Jaxon said. "Is Billy in?"

She nodded. "He's free. Go on in."

Jaxon passed her desk, entering the office to the right. His old high school buddy Billy Palmer—a real estate agent two years his senior—was behind his large desk. Billy had been scouted for the NFL before a knee injury ended his career.

"Jaxon, this is unexpected," said Billy cheerfully, gesturing to a chair for Jaxon to sit in. "What can I do for you?"

After putting down his coffee cup on the small table next to the chair, Jaxon got straight to the point. "Tell me you didn't know what these ladies were going to turn the bar into."

Billy shifted in his seat and raised his hands defensively. "They never mentioned anything about a cocktail lounge to me," he claimed. "I thought they planned to keep things the same. I only realized something was up when they began renovations."

Jaxon ran a hand through the scruff on his face. "Is there nothing we can do? Say something to them so they'll go back to the laid-back Western bar everyone loved?"

Billy gave him a crooked smile as he placed both hands flat on his desk. "Have you met the ladies?"

"I have," Jaxon answered with a firm nod.

"Then I think you're quite aware that they aren't meek and mild," Billy replied dryly. "I've already learned that lesson. If you want to tell them how to run their bar, go right ahead."

Jaxon snorted. "Marriage has softened you up, buddy."

Billy chuckled. "Nope, it's made me smarter. I know when it's best to keep my mouth shut. Good luck getting them to change their minds."

Again, Jaxon snorted, shaking his head. "Fine, I'll handle this on my own." He rose and grabbed his coffee cup before adding sarcastically, "Scaredy-cat."

Billy kept laughing as Jaxon headed for the door. Before he stepped out, he turned back to Billy. "If I can't convince them, what can I do to buy back the bar?" He needed to fix this. The townsfolk loved Timber Falls. They loved the small-town feel. They loved the rustic experience, the country music, the dancing and the great beer. The *new* Naked Moose had none of those elements.

Jaxon had a heavy heart as he thought about how his bar was no longer brightening up the town. He'd brought something unique and special to the area—a lively hangout spot, a cozy refuge, a place where anyone could laugh, dance and let loose. Now that was all gone. This new bar catered to the tourists, not those who lived and loved the town.

He was so damn mad at himself. He'd been so busy filling his father's boots since his death to save his family's legacy, he suddenly realized *his* legacy was being threatened. He'd brought life, good music and great people to Main

Street. This new bar brought fancy drinks, luxury and pop music. All things that were great—just not in Timber Falls. He wouldn't let Charly, no matter how drawn he was to her, ruin the special place he'd created to bring the town together. A place, considering how annoyed some people were, that meant a lot to them.

Billy lifted his brows at Jaxon's question. "You really want to buy the bar back?"

Jaxon nodded. "If it means correcting a mistake I've made, then yes." He'd have to drain his savings and use his inheritance to hire staff to run the bar in his absence, but what choice did he have?

"Well, if you mean that," Billy said, leaning back in his chair, folding his arms, "you'd have to cover their renovations and offer them more than what you sold it for to make it worth their while to move to a new location. Do you want me to talk to them?"

Jaxon smacked his hand against the door frame. "Leave it for now. Let me see if I can get them to change their minds about their vision."

Billy snorted. "Good luck with that."

Jaxon ignored Billy's doubt and headed for the front door. "Nice to see you, Sara."

He got a glare in return. "Goodbye, Jaxon," Sara muttered.

Sighing, he exited the office and hit the road again, unsure what he'd done to deserve a glare.

On his way back home, he tried to think of a way to steer

Charly toward making the regulars happy by not turning the bar into something so…*big-city*.

A plan began to form in his head over dinner, and by the time he picked up Gunner and Eli to head back into town, he'd decided that a delicate approach was probably the best way to present the situation.

Charly simply needed to get to know him and life in Timber Falls, and then she'd realize what she was taking away from the town by not keeping the bar Western themed.

On the drive back to the bar at twenty minutes to eight at night, Jaxon drove easy down the country road when he noticed someone waving at them from a pulled-over truck off to the side.

"Oh, shit," Eli agreed from the back seat.

"It's Lee," Gunner said. Lee was Isabella's husband.

"That doesn't look good," Jaxon said. His truck's engine revved loud as he hit the gas pedal.

Lee was waving wildly when Jaxon finally reached him. He slammed his truck to a stop, threw it in Park and hopped out, running to Lee.

Lee's face had drained of color and his lips were pressed into a thin line, like he was about to be sick. His hands shook and his voice quavered. "Isabella's in labor. She won't make it to the hospital. I forgot my cell phone—" He looked around frantically, clearly struggling to keep his composure despite the fact that he had no idea what to do next.

Isabella let out a screech, prompting Jaxon to glance over his shoulder at Eli. "Call 911." He looked to Gunner. "Grab one of my sweaters from the back." He rushed toward the passenger side of the car.

Isabella was lying sideways across the armrest, halfway out of the car. Jaxon placed a hand on her arm. "I didn't mean you should have the baby *now*," he said lightly, trying to ease her worries.

She screamed, her face pinching. "He's coming."

"Don't push, Isabella," Jaxon said firmly. "Don't push."

She began shoving her pants down. "He's coming. He's coming."

Not even a few seconds later, Jaxon found himself holding a newborn in his hands while a wave of emotion rushed over him. He wrapped the infant in the sweater Gunner handed him just before emergency services arrived and took over from there.

He stepped back, accepting the wipes the paramedic offered him, and cleaned himself up.

By the time he was done, they were loading Isabella onto the stretcher. She reached for Jaxon's hand. "Thank you, Jaxon. Thank you."

"Congratulations," he replied, squeezing her hand tight. "You did great, Mama."

She gave him a teary smile, before her eyes darted to the baby nestled in her arms. He felt a strange tightness in his chest before accepting Lee's embrace. The happiness radiating from them only reminded him how dark his days had been since his father had passed away.

He missed that feeling of a family. If he didn't have Gunner and Eli, he knew facing that truth would likely drown him.

Once Lee hopped into the ambulance, it took off with sirens blaring toward the hospital, and Gunner drove off with Lee's car while Jaxon followed closely behind them.

Images of Isabella and Lee looking at each other with love on their faces filled his head, something which made his chest tighten. He'd never felt love like that with any woman, so blindly clear to anyone who saw it, and so powerful it could make a man weak at the knees.

After Gunner left Lee's car in the hospital's parking lot, with the keys hidden above the visor, they hit the road again. He hoped Charly forgave him once she understood why he was forty minutes late. But when he entered the bar—Charly waiting near the entrance and casting him a stern look—he knew that was doubtful.

"You're late," she stated, folding her arms across her chest.

"I know, I'm sorry." He drew closer in awe of her unyielding stare. Men twice his age weren't half as fierce. Even with the annoyance in her eyes, she looked more radiant than the previous day. She was wearing a lacy white dress with high heels and had done her hair straight with extra makeup to emphasize her beautiful eyes. "Can you forgive me?" he asked.

She scrutinized him before asking suspiciously, "Depends. Why were you late?"

"He just delivered a baby on the side of the road," Eli said flatly.

Charly blinked in surprise at him. "You delivered a baby?"

Gunner encouraged her further, nudging her arm with his. "Don't be too hard on him, Charly. He did good tonight."

Jaxon couldn't break away from her gaze as her entire demeanor shifted from puzzlement to something else entirely. "How about we drop this topic and move on to that drink you promised me tonight?" he asked her.

His only goal tonight was getting her to soften toward him and to show her what this bar meant to everyone in town. His dream, *his bar*, was burning to the ground around him and he had to put out the fire.

Her shoulders tensed slightly. "Listen, I feel terrible about this now since you've obviously had a difficult night so far...but you should understand that I thought...well... I heard you like to play games with women...so, um..." She heaved out a sigh and stepped back slightly. "I was annoyed with you after yesterday, so I intended to teach you a lesson about playing games."

The moment she stepped out of the way, thunderous applause erupted from the throng of women filling the bar. Jaxon glanced up to see a banner strung over the bar reading Forget your crappy ex-boyfriend. Win yourself a date with a real cowboy!

Eli drawled, "Oh, hell."

Gunner howled with laughter.

Jaxon couldn't believe his eyes. Obviously, they had expected his arrival tonight. He then focused on the woman who had played him like a fool. "Rather than having drinks with me tonight, you actually planned to auction me off?"

Charly flinched, her face turning pink. "I was just playing the game before you did. You can say no. I won't hold it against you, and I'll find another cowboy for the date."

He stared at her incredulously, amazed by her boldness even as he noted the banner was raising money for Haley's Place—a shelter for women who had been abused. He had never taken part in anything like this before, but as he looked into Charly's bright eyes, he wondered if maybe he should have. The cause was a good one. Doing this for charity was one thing, but having an opportunity to even the score against Charly was too tempting to pass up.

"Damn," he muttered with a grin. "Looks like I've been outplayed." Turning to her fully, he added, "I'll do this, but starting tomorrow, stock some craft beer for the regulars who supported this place before you took it over."

She frowned. "Why do you care about having beer here so much?"

"Because I owned this place before you."

Her eyes widened. "Oh."

Of course, she wouldn't have known that. Jaxon had made the bar a corporation when he'd opened it. So when he'd sold the property, it was under the business name.

She looked him up and down as she contemplated his proposition. "What if I refuse to this agreement?"

"Then I won't take part in whatever grand scheme you're

devising, and it will fail. I don't think you want your first event to fail. Right?"

She narrowed her eyes into slits. Obviously, she knew he had her cornered. After a long, tense moment, she held out her hand in agreement. "Deal."

A spark flared between them, storming heat into his groin. By the darkening of her cheeks, he knew he wasn't the only one to feel this unexplainable energy pulling them together.

When their hands separated, she grabbed the microphone from behind the bar and switched it on. "Ladies, get ready to bid for Jaxon Reed. Come on, cowboy, show us what you've got."

Jaxon shook his head slowly, grinning back, feeling like he'd been bested, but for once, he liked it. Though he also had no intention of going on a date with someone he wasn't asking himself. He leaned over to Gunner, discretely grabbed his wallet from his pocket and whispered in Gunner's ear, "Give what's in there to Janessa." She had a serious boyfriend and would have no interest in this date. "There is only one woman I want to win this date."

Gunner chuckled, accepted the wallet and gave a nod. "Got it."

Jaxon then followed Charly as she got onto the bar and readied himself for whatever absurdity awaited.

Charly kept her gaze on him as he hoisted himself up onto the bar as if expecting him to relish every second of the moment, and he didn't understand it. She hadn't even met him before. Evidently, somebody had told her that he enjoyed his bachelorhood too much. But those days were far behind him now. Women just didn't get that when he started the bar business, work came first. He couldn't blame them for not wanting to take second place. Then after his father had passed away, he'd been lost in a foggy stupor when it came to dating and drowning in his sorrows. But he had never made any promises to anyone; he knew that for certain.

He began to wonder what had happened in Charly's life that made her think the worst of a man without even knowing him.

He cast his gaze out over the gathering of women and he spotted Gunner chatting with Janessa. She smiled, caught his eye and nodded, and Jaxon exhaled a breath of relief. The last thing he needed was a date he did not want. He didn't recognize anyone in the crowd, telling him all these women came from out of town. He suspected Charly had posted this on social media, which brought in a crowd. No one in town cared about dating a real-life cowboy. It was simply a way of life.

Charly stepped forward and addressed the crowd, saying, "Ladies, thank you for coming here tonight to support Haley's Place. We have a genuine real-life cowboy up for auction tonight." She then turned her attention to Jaxon and asked, "Jaxon, what kind of evening do you have planned for your date next Friday?"

Obviously, she intended to really put him on display and thought he'd fail at coming up with a good date. He grinned devilishly at her. "We'll start off at my ranch, where I'll cook dinner for you," he told the crowd. "Afterward, we'll get on our horses and ride out to the mountains so that we can watch the sunset before staying a bit longer to stargaze as we make our way back in the moonlight. How does that sound?" he asked the crowd of eager women.

Cheers filled the room, but if he listened closely, he could hear Eli and Gunner barely containing their laughter behind them.

Charly looked taken aback by Jaxon's answer, making him question again what she'd heard about him. She cleared her throat. "All right, ladies, let's start the bidding at fifty dollars. Call out your name before you make your first bid."

Jaxon began to feel like cattle as the woman threw out bids, going higher and higher, with Janessa topping each one.

Until the bidding got to twelve hundred dollars.

Charly said, "Twelve hundred? Going once? Twice? And the winner of the date is… Janessa!" she called.

Jaxon breathed a long, slow sigh of relief.

Applause echoed through the bar until it was silenced by Janessa, who said, "But I'm afraid I can't go on the date. I've got a boyfriend."

"Oh," Charly said in surprise.

"I want to give it away to you, then," Janessa suggested.

Jaxon had difficulty concealing his grin as Charly's eyes thinned and her stern gaze settled on him. "Is that so?" she remarked icily.

"Yes," Janessa answered before Jaxon could open his mouth.

Cheers shook the bar this time from all the excitement watching this show unfold.

With everyone looking her way, Charly swept her glance across the room and gave them a smile. "Thank you for your support for Haley's Place and to The Naked Moose." She hopped off the bar soon after and music filled the room again as everyone started singing and dancing.

Once he jumped down as well, Charly faced him and scowled. "You cheated."

He shook his head. "No, I simply played your game and won."

Her eyes narrowed as she placed her hands on her hips. "What are you up to now?"

"Not up to anything," he said and flashed a grin. "But it looks like we're going on a date."

She stared him down, until she returned the smile with a sly one of her own. "You do realize that I've outsmarted you once already. Who's to say I won't do it again and get out of this date?"

He chuckled, leaning in closer, catching the fresh aroma of her floral perfume. He shouldn't engage her—she was ruining his bar and she appeared to think the worst of him—and yet, he fought against the desperate urge to pull her into him. "Sweetheart, I'd say I'd be disappointed if you didn't try to outsmart me again."

Heat flared in her eyes. "Game on, cowboy."

Four

Six days had passed since the auction night, and Charly still felt a warm glow from the twelve hundred dollars they raised for the shelter. Willow delivered the check, and Charly was swarmed with a sense of relief knowing that helping other women who had gone through what Willow had was helping her heal. Willow's abusive ex-boyfriend, Niko, was still in jail, and Charly hoped it would stay that way without him finding out that Willow had moved to Timber Falls.

Rolling into the weekend again should have brought excitement, but frustration weighed on Charly's chest like a lead brick. No matter that they brought in craft beer after she made the deal with Jaxon, the locals were still less than thrilled with their efforts. And she had no idea how to make any of them happy, which grated on her every last nerve. She hated this self-doubt rising up telling her: *you have no idea what you're doing and Marcel would have had this problem solved already.* The word on the street was that the bar was a disappointment, and that simply could not do.

Seated at her desk in her office just off the small kitchen at the back of the bar, she knew she had to fix this. The bar could not fail. She couldn't even consider it, because even she knew that she was barely treading water to stay afloat. Marcel had made most of the decisions with the bar they had owned, so if their endeavor in Timber Falls failed, it would mean she'd failed romantically *and* professionally too.

She needed a win. And she needed it badly.

Shaking the darkness that hung like a shadow away, she went through this week's deliveries and menu items, making sure that she had everything Aubrey needed for the week ahead.

Right then, her cell phone beeped indicating a text message. She scooped it up next to her laptop and looked at her phone. Her heart promptly sank at Marcel's text.

Charly, I'm begging you—please call me.

Why won't he leave me alone?

She considered answering his text or possibly calling him. Maybe he deserved that much. Maybe he'd realized the mistake he made, and he'd give her some epic apology that would heal the fractures in her heart. The truth was, not only had he ruined her emotionally, but he'd also taken a financial toll on her too. She had wanted to break her connection with him, so rather than make him sell the lucrative bar they owned and divide the profit, she asked him for repayment of her original investment and made a clean break.

She didn't regret it then. And she didn't now.

Nothing he could say would fix any of this. She didn't want an apology. She didn't want an explanation. She wanted him to suffer, and if that meant ignoring him, then so be it. She left her phone alone and buried herself back into her work.

A solid plan that got her through her to-do list. She wrapped up her emails in the office, confirming the details for the divorcee's party that was coming up on the weekend.

She was about to stand and head back into the bar, hearing the voices getting louder as the bar was thankfully getting busier, when her phone buzzed on her desk. She grabbed it, immediately recognizing her mother's name on the screen.

"Universe, give me strength," she mumbled before pressing the green answer icon. "Hi, Mom."

"Hi darling, how are you?" Her mother's voice sounded as fierce as ever over the line.

"I'm great," Charly said, not wanting to get into a full explanation of her current situation about a bar that was not taking off like her one back in Phoenix did.

"That's good to hear," Mom said.

Before Charly could say more, her father's gentle voice suddenly filled the line. "Hi, Jelly Bean. Miss you."

The warmth of his love washed over her, easing the tension along her shoulders. "Miss you too, Dad."

Mom's voice returned like usual, shutting her dad out of the conversation. Not that her mother wasn't a good woman—she was—but she was also strong-willed, opinionated and always thinking she knew what was best for Charly.

Most times, she hadn't a clue.

"We've been thinking about coming for a visit to see you and the girls," her mother said.

Charly shut her eyes a moment, willing calmness. Her mother was one of the reasons she decided to go to school in California and not in Michigan. Charly needed a place to breathe and grow, without her mother hovering over her. "While I'd love to see you, I'm so busy with the bar right now. Perhaps if we could wait a couple months, I can take some time off while you're here. We'll make a vacation out of it."

A long pause followed. A heavy pause that was full of all her mother's worries and then some. "Should we be worried about you? Marcel said you're not responding to him."

"Why are you talking to him?" Charly asked, trying to keep the annoyance out of her voice.

"He feels terrible," her mother said. "You should hear him out."

"He should feel terrible," Charly retorted, leaning back in her chair. "He's the reason I had to walk away from the bar I helped build and why our relationship failed."

"I'm not saying you should forgive him—" her mom started to say.

"Mom, I love you," Charly interrupted, the sternness in her voice leaving no room for argument, "but you didn't see what I did. You haven't walked in on who you thought was the love of your life having sex with someone else."

"I know dear, but to heal you need to face this head on," her mother replied.

Charly bit back the curse words threatening to spill out of her mouth. She didn't blame her mom for trying to fix this problem. Charly had built a life with Marcel. He'd been a part of the family since they began dating in college. Her parents loved him. His had seen her as their own daughter. The breakup wasn't only difficult for Charly, but for all of them. She hadn't heard from his parents since then, but they had been trying to do damage control with her parents. They were standing by their son's side and she could respect that. But there was no reversing the clock now.

"Mom, I love you," Charly said, firming up her stance. "But I don't want to talk about him anymore. I'm moving on with my life. Please stop calling and talking about him."

Her mom's voice grew tight. "All right honey, you're obviously distressed and tired. We'll discuss this later."

No, we won't. "Bye." Charly ended the call. She collapsed her head onto the desk with a loud thump and sighed. She had a new life in Timber Falls she was trying to build, not fix an old one.

When her phone buzzed again, she nearly tossed her phone out of her office, but then she noticed the incoming message.

Hey, it's Jaxon. See you in 30 minutes.

She frowned at her phone, utterly lost at his meaning. She texted back: 30 minutes for what exactly? And how did you get my number?

A cowboy always has his ways. Have you forgotten our date?

Damn, she hadn't actually thought he'd follow through. She hadn't been overly nice to him—why would he want a date with her? Cursing the way her belly fluttered in excitement at the thought of seeing him, she wrote back: I can't go on a date. the bar's too busy.

You're the boss, and there are 3 of you. I'll see you in 30.

She leaned back in her chair and huffed at his lack of taking no for an answer. She wagered Jaxon likely relished the challenge she'd presented him. Men like him—like Marcel— always enjoyed such a pursuit. He probably assumed she was playing hard to get, though that wasn't the case at all. She didn't want the man every woman wanted. She had no intention of going on a date with him.

She decided that the only way to get through to him would be to shake his feathers up a little. She typed: I really don't want to be blunt about this, but since you won't take the hint... I'm on my period and it's really heavy. I've got horrible cramps and going on a horseback riding adventure is the last thing on my mind right now.

She waited for a snappy response, however after a few minutes passed all that greeted her was a quiet phone. She smiled in relief that her plan worked, and Jaxon had finally given up on this wild idea.

With a deep sigh, she powered off her computer and made her way out to the bar, which was busier, but she still got the sense most of the people in the bar weren't locals. Only one booth had cowboy hats hanging on the hooks. One table had a young couple, where both men wore designer clothes. The table next to them had a woman with a Chanel handbag. Farther down, all the women wore fancy sundresses with high heels. All were a telling sign that their social media marketing was working to bring in out-of-towners and tourists, but these weren't the people Charly wanted to impress.

She sighed in frustration. She wanted Timber Falls to become their home, and right now they were so far away from becoming a part of the community.

Back in Phoenix, she had known nearly every business owner on the street. She had good relationships with everyone. Most locals in Timber Falls barely talked to them now. Their morning breakfasts had never been so quiet. When people did talk to them, the conversations were kept short.

As she stepped inside, a quiet hum of conversation filled the air, and soft rock music played in the background. She immediately noticed a few tables were full. At one of the booths, more cowboys sat. Every one of them had a sour expression on their faces.

Charly moved closer to Willow and Aubrey behind the bar and said, "I don't understand why they're so miserable. Jaxon asked us to bring in craft beer and we did." Most people who walked through the bar's doors seemed happy. Some ordered beers. Others tried the cocktails. But there were still some locals that looked less than impressed. "What more do they want?"

Pouring beer from a can into a large glass mug, Willow shrugged and sighed deeply. "I have no idea why they look so grumpy, but I can assure you, we're not getting something right."

"They've been like this since they arrived," Aubrey chimed in, crossing her arms, eying the four men in the booth. "It's almost like they were a little bit happy that we had the craft beer here, but after they took a sip of it, they all shot me a nasty look."

Charly leaned against the bar, shaking her head in disbelief. "Sometimes I think the people in this town are the most complicated people in the world."

Aubrey grinned, amusement twinkling in her eyes. "Still handsome though," she added with a light laugh.

Charly couldn't deny that part. No matter how much she tried, Jaxon kept popping into her mind. The biggest issue was that he reminded her of Marcel. The hot guy. The charming one. The man that made her temperature rise and *want* again. But he also had major commitment issues, even if he did seem like a good guy. Ignoring those red flags before had got her cheated on. She'd never make that mistake again. The next man she dated—she was in no hurry—would only have green flags. And unfortunately, Jaxon wasn't that guy. If only her body got on board with that realization.

"Well, well, look who it is," Aubrey drawled.

Charly followed her gaze toward the front door and her heart skipped a full beat. Somehow Jaxon looked even better than he had yesterday. His jeans were perfectly fitted, his cowboy boots peeking out beneath them. He wore a black cowboy hat and his beard was trimmed, and even from where she stood behind the bar, she swore she could smell how good he smelled—like an earthy spice. The smirk he directed her way told her that he knew she liked what she was looking at.

Dammit!

Steeling herself against his charms, she looked toward his hands and noticed he was carrying a box of chocolates and a knitted teddy bear atop of a heating pad. Those guards she had firmly placed against him began to crumble.

"Sorry for being late for our date, but I had to pick up a few things," he said. Then he looked to Willow and Aubrey. "Ladies."

Her best friends both grinned from ear to ear and greeted him.

Traitors.

Regardless, she was stunned into silence, taking in the items he brought. She almost felt herself melt a little, until she remembered the warning she'd received about Jaxon. Players knew how to play the game well. It was clear Jaxon was a damn expert, and he intended to win because she'd made it difficult for him.

Two could play this game…

Aubrey broke the moment by gesturing to the items in his hands with an arched brow. "What's with the heating pad?" she asked.

"I hear it's an essential tool for a woman on her period," Jaxon explained with a smirk.

Aubrey blinked. "And you bought them for Charly?"

He nodded.

Willow piped up, "But Charly's not—"

"Thank you for the chocolates and the heating pad," Charly quickly interrupted, fighting against the warming of her face. "They're both thoughtful, but like I said I can't go out tonight, the bar is too busy."

Jaxon scanned the room again, nodding hello to the cowboys in the booth that he obviously knew, before turning back to Charly with that same smirk on his face. "It doesn't seem so busy here," he said teasingly, reminding her that he used to own this place. "Willow and Aubrey could handle things." One slow eyebrow arched. "Or are you reneging on our date?"

Charly took in a shaky breath, trying to quell her erratic heartbeat. Her mind screamed that this was all an elaborate game to Jaxon. A challenge she presented that he needed to conquer. But as she glanced out at the cowboys, who now seemed more settled with Jaxon in the bar—like they cared to be on their best behavior with him there—she began to wonder if he could really help her. The bar had to succeed. And he did own the place before her…

If she lost this bar and failed to make Timber Falls home for all of them, she lost everything, including her dignity.

She had years of experience in knowing what women wanted from a night out, and that knowledge was the reason she got into the nightlife industry to begin with. But she had no familiarity with small-town living or what the locals there desired.

She turned back toward her friends. "Will you be all right if I leave?" she asked.

Willow nodded fervently. "Of course, we'll be fine. Go ahead. Have some fun." She gave Charly a gentle push toward the door.

Aubrey's muttered laughter followed Charly as she stepped forward and allowed Jaxon to open the door for her. He raised an eyebrow again as he stared down at her. "Ready for a good time tonight?"

Charly held his gaze in challenge and returned the smirk. "Not *that* much of a good time," she said, adamant.

Jaxon's mouth twitched, but Charly resisted getting lost in the way his eyes softened with amusement. This evening was about making sure her bar succeeded and they changed the local's minds about them, not losing herself in the alluring charm of this cowboy.

Steeling herself against him, Charly allowed him to lead her away, armed to stay one step ahead of him.

Five

Twenty minutes later, Jaxon walked into his backyard, feeling totally out of his element. He'd dated, nothing too serious to consider marriage, but a couple relationships that lasted a year. Even though this wasn't technically a real date, with Charly it felt almost…*new*, like how a date should have felt like—exciting and almost…nerve wracking. He like how she challenged him and knew nothing about him. She was looking at him through eyes that didn't know the Reed name.

On his back deck, he had laid out some mats and pillows, forming a cozy spot for them to relax together. He'd thought about how he could make Charly feel better while she was on her period. He wasn't sure what she would need, but he wanted to do something kind. He shook his head. Part of him told himself that he was trying to keep Charly and her friends from destroying the bar he had built from the ground up and which had meant a lot to the locals in town…but he knew that wasn't why he had brought her there tonight.

His gaze fell to her face, seeing the surprise in her expression at the date night he'd planned. He felt a warmth fill him, recognizing *this* was the reason that drew him to her. He cared to impress her. Since his father had passed, life had been a blur. He leaned on his friends. He worked hard to fill his dad's role, but nothing had ignited a spark. Until he locked eyes with her and that spark quickly became a roaring flame.

"This is quite the view," she said softly.

He followed her gaze to the pastures where the geldings grazed. The sun was slowly beginning to sink in the west, with a gentle breeze carrying the smell of rich grass. His bay gelding, Altair, who had been bred and born at the farm watched them closely. His brown eyes were gentle as he stared on like he was as curious about Charly as Jaxon was. He smiled back at Charly. "There is only one view better than this."

She slid her warm gaze to him. "What's that?"

He winked. "A pretty woman with this view behind her."

She snorted, flicking her hair over her shoulder, and rolled her eyes. "Does that line really work for you?"

Normally it did. He shrugged, shoving his hands in his pockets. "I don't know you tell me. Did it work?"

She laughed, her expression softening in a way he hadn't

seen yet. "No, it definitely did not." But as she glanced back out to the horses in the pasture, he caught the pinkish hue in her cheeks and felt a spark of hope.

He'd never met a woman that made him work this hard. He liked it. Perhaps there was still a chance that he could make an impression on her after all. "Take a seat and get comfortable and I'll go grab dinner," he said. Before he entered the house, he asked, "Want a drink? Beer, water, sweet tea?"

"Beer sounds great," she said.

Considering she didn't stock beer at the bar, he was surprised she drank it. He gave her a nod and then hurried inside entering his small galley kitchen. He took out the chicken wings on the pan that was being warmed in the oven and switched off the stove, taking everything and placing it all on the serving plate. Before heading back outside, he grabbed the beers from the fridge.

When he found her sitting against the pillows staring out into the pasture with a little smile, he grew even more curious about her. She was a walking contradiction. One minute ready to fight. The next, sweet and soft. "I'm sorry this isn't a homemade meal like I promised, but I didn't have the time. Today was a long day." He put the hot pan down on the wire rack and placed the other pan next to it, setting out the chicken wings, spinach dip, tortillas, and fried pickles—all his favorite things for snacking.

"Where did you order this from?" she asked. "It looks really great."

He cracked a beer and handed it to her. "There's a tiny little place when you come into town, Sparrow Catching. It's got some of the best food in town."

She smiled. "The girls and I go for breakfast every day. We've grown close to Jenna."

"Nice," he said, returning the smile. "Jenna took over the restaurant from her grandmother. It's been around for a very long time."

"I guess a lot of the places in town have been here awhile, huh?"

He waited for her to dip her tortilla chip in the dip before he dug into the food too. "Most, yes, but not all." He ate the chip then added, "Especially since you and your friends have brought in a whole lot of big city into our little town."

"Is that what makes the locals so grumpy?"

He shrugged. "People around here don't like change," he said, dipping another chip into the dip. "Just takes some time for them to get used to something different." While he wanted to continue that line of conversation to put a little country back into their bar, he figured he needed to get to know her better. "Can I ask why you three moved to Timber Falls?"

She finished her bite and smirked. "Not many new people move here?"

"They visit," he said. "As you've already seen I'm sure, we get tons of tourists, but new residents are rare, especially pretty ones."

His compliment brushed right off her. "It's actually a wild story."

"That's all right," he said. "Lay it on me."

She took a long sip of her beer before she spoke again. "Willow, Aubrey and I grew up together. We all met in kindergarten and kind of stuck together like glue. When we were thirteen, we came up with this drawing of our dream place. After college, we took a backpacking trip to Yellowstone, because I found this place and it looked exactly like our drawing. When we came, we made a pact, that if at twenty-eight our lives weren't what we hoped they'd be, we'd move here together and start over."

He began to understand their fierceness. This wasn't just three best friends moving to a new town. This was three best friends that had felt like failures in their lives, and this was one last shot to prove they could make it out alive. He grabbed a chicken wing. "Are you twenty-eight now?"

She nodded. "Our lives weren't what we hoped for, so about ten weeks ago, we decided to fulfill the pact."

"Wow, that's quite the story, and brave of you all. It couldn't have been easy picking up and just walking away from your life," he said.

She grabbed another tortilla and scooped up some of the spinach dip before she took a bite. "Oh, it's not too hard when you find your fiancé with the head bartender screwing on the bar you own together."

"Ouch," he said, licking the sauce from his fingers, suddenly understanding her intensity toward the opposite sex.

He'd hate men too. "Well, that's a valid reason to walk away."

She chewed a minute and then said, "Yeah, it wasn't hard. Willow and Aubrey were looking for a change too, so we jumped ship and here we are."

He'd never cheated on someone or been cheated on, but he could only imagine how the betrayal would burn. "Do you still talk to him?"

She slowly shook her head. "Doing my best not too. Hopefully he'll get that hint soon enough."

An irrational jolt of jealously stormed through him. "What's his name?" That way if he ever met him, he'd know the type of person he was dealing with.

"Marcel."

"And you owned a bar together in…?"

"Phoenix. We bought it right after college."

A horse neighed off in the distance as he asked, "So, it's a different type of place than what you have now."

"Very different," she said. "I always knew I wanted to get into the bar industry. I bartended all through college and could just see myself working in that line of work. But the nightclub was more of Marcel's idea. Not that I didn't have input and worked damn hard to get it up and running, but the dance club was his idea."

"What you have now is more in line with what you wanted?" he asked.

She nodded. "Smaller. More intimate. A place for friends and fun. That's what I always imagined I'd have."

"I can understand that," he said. "I liked that about the place too."

"It's a nice place," she said, dipping another chip. "Just needed a little freshening up."

He let the dig roll off, knowing that in her eyes that was exactly what it needed. He didn't feel the need to remind her that small-town people dislike big change. They loved the old, rustic feel of a town they cherished. They loved the country music they grew up on. They loved the old bar. "All right, so let me know if I got this right. You left the big city, leaving a cheating fiancé behind for a small-town with a legend that anyone that moves here finds love."

She laughed. "I didn't know about the legend until the other day, and it's silly anyway."

He agreed with a nod. "I'm not a believer either."

A snort of derision escaped her lips, as if he had just proven her assumptions about him. It was clear she had put him into the same box as her ex-fiancé. He shouldn't have been affected by it—usually he wouldn't have been—but this time he was.

He had eaten two chicken wings in the time she ate one, and the sound of rustling grass cleared his mind. Though he didn't mind when she disrupted the calmness—he actually enjoyed hearing her voice—as she asked, "All right, you heard about my experience into the bar industry. Tell me, why did you sell the bar? It seemed like it was thriving with all the regulars you had, who are dead set on letting me know I'm getting it all wrong."

He chuckled, finished his sip of his beer, and lowered his bottle to the serving plate. "I worked so hard for that bar since I was a young. I knew exactly what I wanted to do with my life, and I created it from the ground up. I saw so much potential for the bar to bring people together; to play pool or line dance, or just enjoy some great beer after a hard day. It was my passion, and I put blood, sweat and tears into the bar."

"Then what happened?" she asked.

He sighed deeply, feeling a familiar ache rise in his chest. "My dad passed away six months ago. Everything changed then and I didn't have a choice but to walk away from the bar to ensure the ranch's success."

She paused, midway lifting her chicken wing to her mouth. "Gosh, Jaxon, I'm so sorry for your loss."

"Thank you," he said. "But my father lived life on his own terms. He ate whatever he wanted and smoked more than any man should smoke. In the end, his heart gave out while he was here on the ranch doing exactly what he loved."

She gave a tight-lipped smile. "There's something beautiful in living life on your terms."

"Yeah, there is." And he respected his dad for it, only he'd choose healthier choices for his life.

She was quiet for a comfortable moment before she spoke again. "So, you gave up your dream for the ranch then?"

"I'm a third-generation horse breeder," he explained with a nod. "Even with the bar, I still spent countless hours here training horses, deciding on breeding lines and continuing with my family's legacy. Dad handled the business aspect while I focused on the training. But when he passed away, there was obviously only one option: I had to step up and take his place so our family tradition could continue."

"But what about your own ambitions? You had to sacrifice them for this."

He didn't hesitate. The answer had always been crystal clear to him. "My dad took care of me after my mom passed away when I was just a kid. He made sure I had everything I'd ever need or want growing up. To pay him respect and keep the family name alive, it wasn't even a question that I should move into the ranch and carry on in his place. When I have kids of my own someday, I hope they can understand why this ranch is so important and why it must be kept going."

"Kids?" she asked incredulously, and then her face settled back into a blank stare. "That's unexpected for a man who is known for breaking hearts in this town."

He merely shrugged in response, not commenting on being a heartbreaker since he didn't feel the need to defend himself. He hadn't broken any hearts he'd known of. "I haven't ruled out the possibility of having a family one day, no matter what anyone around here might think of me.

"And you? Kids in your future?"

Her breath hitched and she glanced down. "Once I thought so, but not—" her voice grew thick with emotion "—not anymore."

To his surprise, he itched to take her hand and ease that pain he saw so plainly on her face. He'd felt a familiarity in her heartache. Not that he'd had a relationship fail, but he'd had a dream die. He'd dealt with that loss in casual relationships and more than a few drunken nights. Until his loss faded into a comfortable peace of acceptance with his new role. But as he looked at her, he suddenly felt like even he was still clouded in the darkness of loss.

She lifted her head, revealing eyes drenched in heartbreak.

He held her gaze, feeling like he was starting to understand her better. "Sometimes things don't work out the way we would like them to," he said, "but that doesn't mean the new path isn't going to be even better."

She studied him intently before saying something which caught him off guard, "You know, you are not at all what I expected you to be."

His brow winged up. "Is that a good thing or bad?"

She didn't even flinch, and said softly, "I'm still deciding."

He figured when it came to this woman that was a win if he'd ever seen one.

Six

As the sun set, the bright glow of a golden orange splashed with pink over the ranch faded as night settled in and the lights flickered to life around the deck. Charly found herself feeling comfortable in a way she hadn't felt since she walked in on Marcel destroying their dream of forever. Since they moved to Timber Falls, she'd been pushing hard to somehow find herself again in the ashes of her old life. As she watched the horses in the fields, the silence brought a sense of peace and calm to her chest which she hadn't realized she was missing.

Seated next to Jaxon on the blanket and pillows, her belly was full and warm from the food and the alcohol. The more time that went by, the more she realized Jaxon wasn't only a handsome face and a body of pure, hard, *delicious* muscle, he was clearly a man who was proud of his family's name, a hard worker, thoughtful, and from what she'd seen so far, a good man.

By the end of the night, she could hardly believe how great the not-so-real date had been. Jaxon hit every mark. He was easy to talk to and highly emotionally intelligent. Plus, he managed to offer sympathy and even moments of righteous anger toward Marcel without making her feel like less than.

She didn't want to admit that he had won her over in spite of herself. But the moment that thought crossed her mind, anger rose. She was again falling into the very trap Marcel had placed her in.

Unable to stop herself, she bristled. "Am I just some game to you?"

Jaxon looked surprised, caught off guard by her sudden outburst. He set his beer bottle down. "What are you talking about?"

"I was warned that you're a heartbreaker," she continued. "That to get involved with you was a huge mistake. After hearing what's happened to me with my ex-fiancé, are you so cruel as to keep on this charade that you're this incredible guy? Why exactly am I here?"

"That's a good question, and one I've been asking myself," he said, holding her stare intently. "But let me address that first comment." He turned a little, leaning one arm against the pillow with his legs stretched out. "This isn't a charade. The only people who really know me are Gunner and Eli. Anyone else in town who says they do is lying.

Yes, I've taken women to my bed. Yes, I've had more casual relationships than serious ones. But I've never promised a woman anything. If that makes me a bad guy, then I suppose I'm guilty."

Charly studied him carefully, looking for any sign of deceit. "So, you're telling me all this wasn't an attempt to get into my pants and prove a point?"

He lifted an eyebrow. "That wasn't my plan, no." A long pause as his steady gaze held hers. "I admit, at first, I wanted to get in your good graces to get you to change your mind about the beer, because I had pissed-off people breathing down my neck."

She frowned. "They called you?"

He nodded. "The locals were used to the bar the way I had it. If one thing could be said about the people of Timber Falls, it's they don't like change. But your little *event* helped me there." Leaning in, he closed the distance and said, "I'd reckon if anyone is playing games here, Charly, it's you, and whatever game you want to play, I'm happy to play along."

He held her gaze so tightly that goose bumps rose on her arms as he bit his lower lip, almost as if he were fighting against closing the rest of the distance and sealing his mouth across hers. Her entire body prickled with arousal at the thought of him nibbling at her lips like that. "Are you really trying to tell me that you don't want to kiss me now?" she asked, trying to call out his lie.

A laugh without mirth escaped him. "I never said that— I said I didn't bring you here expecting to get into your pants." His eyes were full of desire as they lingered on her mouth. "Kitten, if you want honesty, then I'll give it to you. I wanted to kiss you the second I saw the flames in those pretty cognac-colored eyes, and you swiped your claws at me." He smiled at her, a gentle but sensual smile that made her guards fall. "The only reason I brought you here to-night is because I feel a spark with you. One I haven't felt in a long time. That's why you're here—to explore that."

She felt her pulse race and her breath become shallow. As he spoke, the truth shimmered through, and without her guards up, she couldn't fight the pull to him. She couldn't run from the emotions waging inside her. She craved joy after so much pain. She wanted to feel alive again, to feel beautiful and sexy and wanted more than she needed logic.

In a rush, she flung herself at him.

He seemed shocked before embracing her tightly. Until he groaned, taking over, and claiming her mouth with his. Their kiss was passionate, intense and everything she sud-denly needed. She didn't even recognize herself as she strad-dled his waist, sending him onto his back, but she needed *this*. To feel wanted instead of feeling discarded. She lowered herself against his solidness pressing against her.

Teasingly, she shifted against him and ground her pelvis into his hardened length and heard a moan pass through his lips as his tongue swiped against hers. When she did the movement again, he latched onto her waist, holding her still. He backed away, his gaze meeting hers with one eyebrow raised in surprise. "Is there something specific you're looking for here, love?"

She ran her hands up his flexing biceps. "You said I'm the only playing games so how about we play another one?"

"Oh?" he asked, sliding his hands back to cup her bottom. "What's the bargain now?"

"I give you one more thing you want at the bar to get your regulars off your back."

His voice lowered. "And what do you want?"

She brought her mouth close to his, inhaling the earthy scent of him, feeling the hardness between her legs. "I want to forget Marcel's touch."

"I could help with that." He grinned teasingly and nuzzled into her neck before speaking in her ear. "Let me remind you that you said you were on your period…not that I'm opposed…"

Her lower lip quivered as she stifled a smile. "I might have misled you on that part…"

He chuckled, low and deep, and planted a gentle kiss on the corner of her mouth and stared into her eyes. "I want more craft beer. Not only one brand, but at least five, and I give you the names."

So that's what earned her scowls? She didn't choose the right brands and she didn't offer enough options. Part of her wanted to recoil that she got this so wrong and didn't consider how much the locals loved their town as it was. But the other part of her cut herself a break. She grew up in big cities. People were more open to change there.

All she knew now was she wanted to make everyone happy that came through the bar's doors. She wanted to belong to Timber Falls too. "Deal."

A sultry smile played at the corners of his mouth before he molded his lips to hers with searing intensity. Jaxon's kiss was unlike any other she'd experienced before. It was soft and tender yet hard and passionate, leaving her breathless and wanting more.

Electricity coursed through her body as she clutched the hem of his shirt and pulled it up over his head. He helped her take it off and then did the same with her blouse and bra. The breeze brushed across her and she wasn't thinking about anything except how amazing his touch was as his hands cupped her breasts. She moaned and threw her head back, tangling her fingers into his hair while his tongue teased one tight peak and then the next, sending sparks of pleasure all the way down to her toes.

Until she couldn't handle how incredible he felt beneath her hands. She needed to touch him, over every inch of his tight body and rock-hard muscles.

She broke away, scooting further down his legs and reached for his belt. His skin was perfection—smooth, tanned flesh stretched over his honed physique. And with each article of clothing removed, it made her want to lick and kiss him all over again. As if in response to the need inside her, his thick erection hardened even more between her fingers as it sprang free from his pants. She ached in anticipation, her inner walls clenching at the very thought of him stretching her fully, filling her until they both reached completion.

In her hesitation, he fisted himself while staring at her expectantly, almost daringly…a primal challenge in his gaze that heated the blood pooling low in her belly. Her breath stalled in her lungs as she watched him stroke himself. She was sure she had never seen anything sexier until she lifted her eyes to his and caught the intensity burning there.

He lifted an eyebrow at her, giving her a wicked smile. "Pretty sure this is what you wanted, Charly?"

She held his stare, accepting the challenge. "You're right. I did want that." She bit her lip as she slid her hands down his toned body. With one hand splayed across his hard abs, she wrapped her other around his erection and took over the long, slow strokes. That's when he closed the gap between them and kissed her hungrily. He tasted of hot pleasure and sweet satisfaction.

Soon enough, though, his lips weren't enough to satisfy her need and she started kissing her way down his body, exploring every ripple with rapt attention until she reached the V of his waistline. His low groan sent a thrill through her, but it was her own hiss that propelled her forward as she took him into her mouth.

She pulled back, the first salty taste of him still on her tongue. Wanting to drive him wild, she ran her hands along his body as she twirled, stroked, licked and teased him until his moans quickened and his muscles tensed.

Strength flooded through her. She'd felt so out of control lately, but not now. Now she had the power. She had this strong cowboy at her fingertips...and she relished the way he was at her mercy.

She continued, working her mouth and hand together, earning deep grunts.

Until he cursed under his breath and lifted her from him, before his urgent and passionate kisses consumed her. Planting an arm around her waist, he flipped their positions, sliding her beneath him. In a flurry of movements, he had her skirt and panties off.

Kneeling between her legs, he stared at her sex wet with arousal with an intensity that had her heart pounding. His gaze then moved up her body until their eyes met. "How are you this fucking perfect?" he asked gently in awe.

She felt all the truth in those words and squirmed under his potent stare. Rather than ravishing her, however, he caressed her from stomach to breasts to neck as if trying to prove she was real.

With a throaty groan, his mouth found hers again and this time the kiss was soft and gentle, yet still full of fire. From her neck down to her ear, he licked and nipped sweet promises of pleasure. When he reached her ear, he whispered, "I'm going to make this sweet body shake."

Her eyes fluttered as he trailed kisses down her body... slowly...until he was between her legs. She trembled as he licked her inner thigh and she let out a gasp before that sound was stolen away as his tongue moved over her clit.

Nothing about his movements was rushed; each one seemed strategically planned to make her moan louder.

She squirmed, thrusting her hands into his hair. "Please... Jaxon."

His low chuckle vibrated against her skin before he brought her clit between his teeth. Then he sucked. She nearly jumped off the blanket when he pinned her with one arm. She thrashed, lost to the pleasure, as he followed through on his promise.

She shook helplessly until she soared into her orgasm.

When the fog lifted from her mind, she realized he held on to one hip possessively. She heard his deep grunts and forced herself to open her eyes, discovering him kneeling between her thighs. He stared down at her like she was his gift. She raised her hand to caress his thigh, as he stroked himself, pleasure tightening every muscle in his body.

With a deep groan, he tossed his head back, pushed forward and quivered through his climax onto her stomach.

She felt lost to the satisfaction simmering through her as he took one of the napkins and cleaned off her stomach. Her mind felt quiet in a way it hadn't been in so long when he gathered her close to his chest. Until his finishing sent confusion racing through her mind. "No sex?" she asked.

He pressed a soft kiss to her neck, a solid wall of muscle behind her. "I'm giving you no ammunition to think that sex is all I want from you."

She felt like that should register...*something*. Her body began to cool, her mind slowly filling with thoughts that she had officially lost her mind, until the chill wasn't only in her body, it was deep in her soul. What was she doing?

Her chest suddenly felt like a vice under the swell of confusion. She'd only just broken things off with her fiancé—the man she planned to spend the rest of her life with—ten weeks ago. Sure, he cheated, but she had never been intimate with someone without love before. She had always needed a connection to let her guards down enough for someone to see her naked. She'd only had two sexual relationships. Her first boyfriend who she only got to second base with, and Marcel.

I need to get out of here…

As the long minutes ticked by, she pretended she was sleeping and waited until Jaxon's long day hit him and his breathing became steady, indicating he was sleeping soundly, before carefully sliding out of his arms. Gathering all the clothes scattered around their makeshift bed, she glanced back one last time. For a moment, she thought of snuggling back up to him, basking in the warmth of his hold…the strength of it.

But reality brought her crashing down—she didn't need a man's comfort right now; she needed to focus on her dreams, and she hadn't even begun healing from Marcel's betrayal. The last thing she wanted was to get so caught up in Jaxon that she decided to change the bar *for* him and not because she thought it was best for the bar. She'd been there and done that before. And there just wasn't enough room for a relationship in her life.

When she had finished her escape around to the side of

the house, she put on her shoes and was startled by a loud
snort. She looked to see a big brown horse with a white
mark shaped like a star on its head. "Oh, don't you dare
judge me," she told the horse.

It gave another snort, and she realized that even the horse
knew how bad an idea this night had been.

She hurried forward, opened the Uber app on her cell and
ordered a car, hoping that Jaxon wouldn't wake up within
the ten minutes it took for the car to arrive. As she made
her way down the long driveway, she sent a message to Willow and Aubrey in their group chat: I'm on my way home.

Willow replied instantly: Is that all you're going to say?!
How'd it go?

Charly texted back: I officially hate cowboys!

Aubrey's response came quickly: Why because that cowboy charmed you right into his bed?

There was no point trying to keep this secret from her
best friends. They would know immediately when she got
home, and they never kept secrets from each other.

Charly cursed and replied: I think it's time for professional help.

Willow sent a stream of emojis that indicated shock, ad-
miration and surprise.

Aubrey replied: Stop! Nothing wrong with a rebound. Especially one that's way hotter than you're ex.

Charly sighed, an incredibly long sigh, heading down
the driveway toward the road. Maybe there was a good
therapist in town...

Seven

Charly was up bright and early the next morning and headed for the bar, even though it wasn't scheduled to open for another four hours. She threw herself into cleaning, stocking shelves and working furiously to avoid thinking about last night with Jaxon. The conversation between her and her friends when she'd come home continued to weigh heavily on her mind.

"Do you like him?" Willow questioned while tucked into the corner of Charly's bed.

Charly plopped down on her mattress and snuggled up in her blankets. "Probably more than I want to."

On the bed beside them, Aubrey stared at Charly for a moment before asking, "Why are you saying that like it's a bad thing to like an obviously good guy from the looks of it?"

"Because I've done this before," Charly said. "I'm not repeating my old mistakes. Yes, he's a nice guy, but there's some obvi-

ous commitment red flags there. Besides, we have a dream to make happen here. Finding a guy isn't part of that dream. Hell, I'm still not over the last guy." Or the future she thought she'd have with Marcel. That was the hardest part in all of this. She needed to stay focused on creating a new future that she could find pride in.

Willow replied, "So then why did you let last night happen?"

Charly hesitated, but then spilled her heart in the one place she wouldn't get judged. "His attention felt…good. He started talking about a spark he felt between us and looking at me all sexy, and I just…kissed him."

Aubrey burst out laughing. "Couldn't help yourself, huh?"

Charly shook her head but couldn't find any amusement. "Have I lost it?" she asked seriously. "Do you think I'm going through some crisis? I have never done anything like that before. I legit grabbed him and kissed him."

Aubrey snorted. "I'm pretty sure you got exactly what you needed tonight. Stop feeling bad about it."

Charly looked to Willow. She'd tell her the truth.

Willow just shrugged. "Maybe a little sexy fun is exactly what you need. From what we heard that cowboy is very good at that."

"Oh, hell no," Charly countered, "Last night will never, and I mean, never happen again."

Aubrey raised her eyebrows skeptically. "Why does that sound like you're trying to convince yourself?"

"Because I am," Charly stated, dead serious.

Thoughts of Jaxon stayed with her all morning and into the afternoon. She couldn't deny the spark he was speaking about. She felt it too, right down to the tips of her toes.

But sparks led to fireworks and that sometimes led to love, and getting involved with a heartbreaker was not on her to-do list.

Though those sizzling touches of his lingered on her skin. The passion he exuded clenched her belly tight even now. His low voice brushing her ear sent a shiver down her spine until need was all she knew.

Dammit!

Pushing the heat far, *far* down, she filled a bucket with soap and warm water and started cleaning the baseboards.

She heard Willow's voice suddenly in the bar, startling her out of her trance.

"Don't you think another night with Jaxon would be better than scrubbing baseboards?" Aubrey teased.

Charly glanced away from her cleaning and looked at her best friends. The absurdity of the situation hit her. Here she was on all fours, vigorously scrubbing a baseboard that was already spotless.

"I feel about ready to climb out of my skin," Charly declared before refocusing on the baseboard in front of her. She tossed the rag into the bucket and dropped her head into her hands. "I don't even feel like me right now."

Willow and Aubrey joined her on the floor and held her hands in theirs.

"Of course, you are *you*, and you're wonderful," Willow said soothingly.

Charly gave a weak smile but still felt empty inside. "I

don't like that I can't trust my own mind and my own judgement."

Aubrey frowned. "What do you mean?"

"I can't remember a time in my life when I didn't have a plan," Charly began as a lump started forming in her throat. "I can't think of a time when I didn't have my life laid out and think everything through. I never doubted my instincts. I always loved going out at night and the energy and atmosphere of exciting places. I knew I wanted to bring people together over great food and incredible drinks. Even after college, I had a plan—open a bar with Marcel, get married, have kids..." Tears threatened to escape, but she managed to push through and continue. "Now we're in this new town, surrounded by people we do not understand, and I'm kissing a cowboy that pisses me off and turns me on all at the same time."

Willow's eyes filled with sympathy. "You're just finding your footing again."

"But the ground is so shaky beneath my feet, and I hate Marcel for that," she admitted. Somehow saying those words aloud made a wound in her soul bleed harder. "I hate him for making me feel like I don't have solid roots in the ground anymore."

Aubrey snorted indignantly. "You're not alone in that sentiment."

Charly let out a heavy breath, their hands pressed so tightly that it almost hurt. "Last night I felt so desperate for Jaxon's affection. I wanted to feel beautiful...sexy, even."

She couldn't stop her tears from spilling over now. "Not like a woman that can be thrown away for someone else."

Soon enough she was embraced in a warm hug, and she melted into it.

After a long moment, Willow broke the silence, saying, "If there is something wrong with anyone, it's with Marcel, not you, Charly."

"I agree," Aubrey said.

Charly stayed in the safety of their arms, letting all her pain out. "I feel broken…like I can't decide what's right for me and what's not, and I hate feeling so shaken."

"You're not broken," Willow said, drawing away from the hug. "You're on a path of rediscovery."

Aubrey said, "And we're all on that path with you. You're not alone, Charly. We're all in this together."

Willow nodded firmly. "We'll be here with you through it all. Even when you decide to jump a cowboy and have your way with him."

Charly laughed and wiped her eyes, looking at her two best friends who had always been there for her without fail. "I love you both so much."

Willow smiled softly. "We love you too."

Aubrey nodded in agreement. "We do."

After another hug, Charly picked herself up off the ground. "All right, enough breaking down for one day," she said, forcing a smile. "We're opening in a half an hour. We've got lots to do."

She left her friends behind and headed for her office,

leaving Willow and Aubrey to get to their opening duties. Seated at her desk, she read through her inbox. After the purge of emotions, she realized she didn't regret last night with Jaxon. She had felt beautiful and wanted, and the passion had been addicting, if she was honest with herself.

Perhaps she did need to let herself off the hook. The life she had in Phoenix was over. She was evolving—and maybe that was okay...

Right as that thought slid warmly through her, she heard raised voices coming from the bar area and quickly rushed out of her office.

When she spotted Willow standing next to a booth with trembling hands and fearful eyes while being insulted by one of the cowboys, a fury surged through Charly like never before.

Out of the corner of her eye, she noticed Eli—Jaxon's friend—sliding away from the booth where he'd been sitting alone. Instinctively, she waved him off and marched toward the table with fists clenched tight.

"What's going on here?" she demanded, sliding up to the table.

The cowboy's eyes roved her body, pausing at her breasts before snapping back to her face. "You're doing a crappy job running this place," he said arrogantly.

"Interesting," Charly replied icily. "I don't seem to recall asking for your opinion."

He tried to smirk, but it came off as more of a sneer. "You'll lose customers if you don't listen to me, sweetheart."

His gaze wandered back to her chest, as though it was his right to imagine touching her.

Anger boiled within her as she snapped her fingers in his face with force. "My eyes are up here, buddy," she growled. She pressed her hands against the table as she leaned into his face. "Listen, *sweetheart*," she drawled out sarcastically. "I know we're the only bar in this town. That means we're the only bar you can come to and put your sleazy moves on some desperate woman who can't see how pathetic you are." She watched with satisfaction as the vein in his forehead bulged dangerously. "You've got one chance to apologize to Willow or you can get up and leave and never be allowed back in again. Do I make myself clear?"

The other man at the table coughed, obviously trying to hide his laughter.

The one facing Charly snorted. "I'm just trying to give you some advice."

"We're not asking for any," she said and pulled away from the table, crossing her arms.

He stared her down for a full minute before glancing at Willow. "Sorry, ma'am."

Willow attempted a smile. "It's fine."

But Charly could tell by Willow's trembling and haunted expression that it was anything but fine. She wanted to sock this jerk in the face. "Do you want a beer, or do you want to leave?"

He took a quick look menu. "I'll have the Foxy Diva."

The only craft beer they currently had in stock. "Great,"

she said to him. Glancing to the others at the table, she said, "And for the rest of you?" They all chose the same thing, so Charly nodded. "Coming right up."

She followed Willow and sped her steps until she was standing next to her. "Go take a break at the back."

Willow nodded before rushing off to enter the backroom.

"Is she all right?" Aubrey asked as Charly made it behind the bar.

"Just shook-up," Charly answered before adding exasperatedly, "Why are they always mean to her instead of me?"

Aubrey chuckled. "Because you're intimidating."

Charly grinned softly. "Good." She reached inside the fridge and took out three beers with one hand while observing Eli stand in front of the table in similar fashion as Charly had done earlier.

The cowboy held Eli's gaze but leaned back as if he wanted to stay away. The others sitting around the table and looking on were still, not moving a muscle. She couldn't hear what he was saying, but it was clear Eli wasn't being friendly.

Eli left the table, returning to his seat and his beer and Willow emerged from the backroom with her chin held high.

"Are you okay?" Charly asked, when she sidled up next to her.

"Yeah, I'm fine," Willow replied with a nod. "Just the intensity, you know, it brings me back to…"

To her attack and thirteen stitches…

Charly grabbed Willow's hand and squeezed tight. "Of course, it would."

The clearing of someone's throat grabbed Charly's attention. She turned her head, meeting the jerk who was barely holding their gazes. "It looks like we won't be needing those beers after all," he said while placing four twenty-dollar bills on the bar counter. "This will cover those. Keep the change."

Charly watched as the jerk and his friends left through the front door.

Eli rose and put on his cowboy hat, but his eyes were fixed entirely on Willow as he tipped his hat and then followed the men outside.

"You know," Charly said to Willow and Aubrey once the door was shut behind him. "I take back my earlier statement."

"What statement?" Aubrey said.

Charly smiled. "That I hate all cowboys. I don't hate *all* of them."

Willow started at the closed door. "Yeah, me neither."

Even a hurricane couldn't wake Jaxon, his father used to say. He woke the morning after what he thought was a spectacular night, however, to an annoyingly bright sun, a rash of mosquito bites on his arm and Charly sneaking out on him, which explained why he hadn't felt her leave his arms.

Annoyance dug its nails into him. He reached for his cell phone, but instead of calling her, he composed a text:

Beautiful mornin', minus the part where I woke up and you weren't in my arms.

He waited ten minutes before he admitted to himself that she ghosted him. Despite his declining mood, he cleared off the back deck before showering and getting dressed for the day. Though thoughts of Charly didn't stray far from his mind as he worked through training two horses, updating paperwork in his office and checking in with the cowboys at the ranch. By nightfall there still wasn't any word from Charly so his mood was darker than when he'd awoken.

Jaxon grabbed three beers from the fridge before returning to the porch, where his friends Eli and Gunner were waiting for him. Just as he was about to step outside, he noticed Lee's truck driving up the driveway.

"What's Lee doing here?" Gunner asked as Jaxon handed him a beer. He shrugged and gave one to Eli too.

By the time he set his beer down on the wooden planks of the porch, Lee parked beside the porch and Jaxon spotted Isabella in the back seat. He bounded down the stairs just as she opened her car door.

"You already made it out of the hospital?" Jaxon asked, swinging open her door.

She nodded, getting out of the car as Lee did on the other side.

"We're driving home, but I wanted to make sure we came by."

Jaxon offered her his arm for support, and she stepped closer giving him a hug.

"I can't thank you enough for what you did," she said, squeezing him tight. "I thought Lee was going to pass out."

He laughed quietly, giving her one last squeeze before pulling away. "You're welcome. I'm glad he didn't faint. That I have no experience with."

Isabella smiled, looking exhausted yet overjoyed at the same time.

"Here's our Clementine," Lee beamed, eyes aglow with pride. "Who we thought was going to be a Corey."

He offered the baby to Jaxon, and Jaxon cradled the little one in his arms. She had dark hair just like her mom. "She's adorable."

"Thanks! We're totally smitten," Isabella replied.

Jaxon stared down at the sleeping baby, and he wondered if this would have been his life had he not thought he had all the time in the world in his younger years or devoted so much energy to getting his bar running. It always felt like his father would live forever, and while he was happy living freely in his youth, he didn't look to the future much back then.

A sharp pang of sadness hit him in the chest. His father should have experienced being a grandfather. He would have been a great one. Jaxon attempted a smile and glanced up at Lee and Isabella, their arms around each other while they gazed adoringly at their child.

Jaxon suddenly felt...*alone*.

He had Gunner and Eli, but they weren't *his*. Chosen family, yes, but not something that belonged only to him.

"Thank you for bringing her by," he finally said as he returned the baby to Lee. "I'm glad to see you're both well and on your way home."

Lee headed around the truck, returning the baby to the car seat, while Jaxon helped Isabella back into the car.

She fastened her seat belt and then grinned at him. "Did you ever think that after we broke up, you'd be delivering my baby on the side of the road?"

Jaxon laughed. "Can't say it crossed my mind."

She just smiled. "Consider your coffees on the house for the rest of your life."

Gunner called, "Does that go for me too?"

"No," Isabella said to everyone's laughter.

"Take care," Jaxon said. He rapped the top of the truck's roof and then stepped back as they waved, driving away.

Jaxon made his way back up the porch steps and grabbed his beer as Eli said, "A baby—it's hard to imagine, huh?"

Jaxon agreed with a nod and took a seat in the chair next to Gunner, who him asked, "How'd it go with Charly last night?"

"Great, until she ghosted me this morning."

Gunner's brows shot up. "That's a first."

Before Jaxon took a swig of his beer, he said, "Definitely not something I'm used to."

Eli smirked knowingly. "Karma's catchin' up to ya."

"No doubt about it," Jaxon said after he swallowed. The truth was, he was miffed by the fact that someone was talking about him behind his back. Sure, the last six months he had nothing more than one-night stands, but that was a way for him to escape the pain of losing both his dad and the bar he had built. He had never made anyone promises of a relationship. He'd always been clear that sex was the only thing on the table.

But he knew his battle went beyond that because Charly had been cheated on. He was currently the enemy. He didn't know why he was so invested. She came with emotional baggage from a breakup just over two months ago. She had her back up most times. Most of all, she had bought his bar and was only agreeing to small changes, when Jaxon knew she needed more to appease the locals who had loved the bar the way it was when he owned it. If the bar failed, the town would lose the one place where the younger crowd could come together for a good time in a place that mirrored life in Timber Falls.

He couldn't watch his bar burn to the ground.

But damn that heat between them...those sweet moans... that lush body... Yeah, he couldn't forget any of it.

Jaxon took another swig of his beer as Eli said, "The cowboys were stirring up some trouble at the bar today."

Jaxon glared at him suspiciously. "How do you know that?"

"I stopped by for lunch and overheard them complaining about something or other."

"What were they griping about exactly?" Jaxon inquired.

Eli drank the last of his beer before speaking. "A cowboy from Valley Ranch was really giving it to Willow. I wanted to go and sort it out, but Charly waved me off and she took care of it."

Gunner asked, "What happened?"

"She laid into them properly," Eli said with a smirk. "I bet when they come back again, they'll probably sip a few of those fruity cocktails from the menu to support the new direction of the bar."

Jaxon laughed. "I've tried one of those cocktails and liked it."

Eli nodded. "I drank one today." His mouth twitched. "I can't say I liked it, but I got through it."

Again, Jaxon chuckled. He also knew Eli wouldn't let this go unpunished after what happened to his sister. "You sure you didn't have anything to do with their change of opinion?" he asked.

"I let Charly handle her business." He gave a slowly building smile. "Then I reminded the prick he shouldn't stick around that day and should probably leave a good tip."

Jaxon chuckled approvingly. The Valley Ranch cowboys caused trouble at the bar often, instigating fights. He had no right to get involved now that he didn't own the place, but he'd never stand idly by and watch Charly and her friends get pushed around. "Let me know if they start any more stuff like that."

"You know I will," Eli assured him.

Jaxon took another swig of his beer but couldn't shake off his worries about Charly. Was she all right after today's incident? Was she thinking of him? Why wasn't she reply-ing to his damn message?

He couldn't take it anymore. He'd already learned enough about Charly to know she put on a brave front. But he couldn't stand the thought that she might feel un-settled after being with someone so soon after she ended her engagement.

Having had enough of being left in the dark, Jaxon fin-ished off his beer and placed the bottle back in the empty case near the front door. "I gotta head downtown." He grabbed his keys from his pocket. "See you both later."

Gunner yelled out, "A particular brunette on your mind?"

Jaxon gave a wave in response before climbing into his truck. The drive to downtown only took twenty minutes. Luckily, he found a parking spot right in front of the bar.

The moment he stepped out, he was met with female voices singing. As he moved closer to the entrance, he no-ticed a sign that read: Take a shot. I untied the knot! The last place he wanted to be was inside this place filled with women attempting to help their friend get over a breakup. He opened the door just enough so that Aubrey could see him, then pointed at Charly.

Aubrey smiled and poked her friend's shoulder.

Those captivating eyes widened when they caught sight of him, and he gestured for her to follow him out of there before anyone else noticed him. He leaned against his truck and waited until she joined him outside of the building, the music falling away as the door shut behind her.

Once she reached him, he said firmly, "I don't know about how things are in Phoenix, but when someone texts you, it's rude not to text them back."

She turned away, avoiding his eye contact. "I'm sorry for not answering your messages earlier."

He firmed his voice. "Do you regret last night?"

Her lips thinned. "No."

"Do you always have one-night stands and then ghost the guy?"

"No," she answered without hesitation. "Last night was a one-time thing."

He paused as he digested her response. Somehow, the fact that this casual fling wasn't part of her normal routine made him strangely pleased, as if he was special enough to make her break her own rules. "Did I do something wrong?" he asked, gentler this time.

"Definitely not," she said, her lips curling up at the corners.

"Then why won't you talk to me again?"

She finally looked at him and eyed him intently before dropping a bomb. "I don't trust myself around you."

Jaxon parted his mouth and shut it. A moment later, he finally found his voice. "Why don't you trust yourself around me?"

She folded her arms across her chest and inadvertently accentuated her cleavage. "Isn't it obvious enough? Do I really need to explain it?"

"Yeah, you need to explain it." His gaze stayed fixed on

her face instead of straying lower like his body wanted to do. "Because I don't get it."

"I'm here to get this bar up and running," she said. "I'm *just* off a brutal breakup. And I'm too smart to ignore what I've heard about you." She closed her eyes and drew in a deep breath before opening them again and fixing him with an intense stare. "On top of all that, I'm a spectacular mess right now. While I don't regret last night, it also can't happen again."

He cocked his head. "Because you don't want it to?"

"Because it's just a bad idea."

Holding her stare just as intensely, he asked, "Why?"

Her face flushed and her gaze roamed over his lips. "Because you have red flags."

The spark he'd felt that first day returned, heating up the air between them. It was nothing he'd ever felt before with anyone. He pushed off his truck and closed the distance. He waited for her to take a step back, but when she didn't, he stopped, nearly toe to toe with her. "How do you know I have red flags when you haven't truly gotten to know me?"

"I've heard all about you," she said, breathless. "You have serious commitment issues. That's a huge red flag."

"Who did you hear this from?" he asked. "Women that I may or may not have been with. Women who know nothing of my life or how I feel. Women who have no understanding that the only reason I had one-night stands was because I was mourning the loss of my father and my dream of the bar, and I was desperate to feel something good."

She stayed silent, and in that silence, he understood that she currently felt very similar.

He continued, "I don't want you to be a one-night stand, Charly. I want to get to know you." He saw her guards were up. He understood why. But he was not against using whatever means he had to get his way. "I heard you had some pissed-off cowboys at the bar today."

"We did," she said with a nod.

"It's not going so well for you and the people in town, huh?"

She frowned. "You already knew that."

"You're right, I did," he said with a smile. "I also know how to make this bar run like a well-oiled machine. It's more than what they drink. It's the lifestyle here in Timber Falls. It's what's important to the people. The sense of community and the fun we have together. We've all grown up here—generations of families—and there is a way of life here that your bar is missing."

"I know how to run a bar," Charly defended. "I had a very successful one in Phoenix."

"You know how to run a bar in a big city," he countered gently. "But you don't live in a big city anymore. What's important to people in a big city is not important here."

"It can't be that different," she said. "Nightlife is nightlife. Everyone is just looking for a good time."

He stared at her, giving her a purposeful look of doubting, knowing she'd rise to the challenge. "How about another bargain? Tomorrow is a Sunday, so the bar is closed.

Come to the ranch, spend time with people who live and work here, and I'll show you what your bar is missing and why the locals aren't happy."

"What do I have to do?" she asked.

"Give me time," he said. "Time for you to get to know me, and for me to prove I only have green flags."

He could see it in her gaze that she was sure he'd fail, that the more time they spent together, the more she'd realize he'd mess this up somehow. "That's the deal, then?" she asked.

He nodded and held his hand out toward her. "That's the deal, Kitten. Do you accept?"

He could see her mind working hard. Until she finally shook his hand firmly, maintaining that same intense gaze. "I do, as long as you stop calling me Kitten." She dropped his hand, spun on her heel and headed for the door.

A bark of laughter left his lips as he called after her jokingly, "Then stop hissing at me and I will." When she didn't turn back, he tucked his hands in his pockets and said, "I'll see you at my ranch tomorrow morning, then?"

A determined look crossed her face as she responded to the challenge. "I'll be there tomorrow morning at eight o'clock." she affirmed.

He grinned after her, determined to win her over, no matter what it took.

Eight

"Adorable!" Willow exclaimed, scanning Charly from head to toe as she entered the centuries-old kitchen the next morning.

Charly wasn't sure what to wear for a day at a horse ranch, so she settled on a plain T-shirt and a pair of jean overalls, with her hair pulled up in a high ponytail and minimal makeup, all the while telling herself it didn't matter what she looked like. She had no one to impress, certainly not a devilish cowboy.

Seated at the breakfast bar, Aubrey took one look at Charly and let out a laugh. "You look like a country bumpkin, but it looks good on you!"

Charly glanced down at herself and sighed. "Why did I agree to this again?" Besides her pride, of course.

"So, we can find our way in this town and make every-

one want to come to the bar," Willow offered. "We're trying to make this our home."

"And because this bar can't fail," Aubrey added. "We have
put all our money into this place. Everything is on the line."

Charly huffed. "Right. That's why." She hated how persuasive Jaxon was. One second, she had things fully in control. The next, she was agreeing to this new deal.

The truth was, he was right. She needed to understand
the locals better if the bar was going to succeed, so she'd
swallow her pride to learn from Jaxon. She hadn't expected
the push back on bringing a little big-city luxury to the
small-town, and it was becoming increasingly obviously
the place meant something special to them.

And they'd ruined it.

It was a hard pill to swallow, but the truth stared at her
hard in the face. She knew nothing about small-town living in Montana and the people who lived there.

She heaved another sigh before grabbing a to-go mug,
then adding some coffee and sugar.

Aubrey raised an eyebrow. "Let's not forget too that this
has *nothing* to do with a certain sexy cowboy."

"I'm doing this for us," Charly countered. "To learn from
him what we're doing so wrong. That's it. That's all. No
funny business." All she needed to do was keep her wits
about her today. Then she'd have what she needed to ensure they got on everyone's good side in town.

Willow leaned against the counter, eating a blueberry

muffin and giving a little shrug. "It doesn't hurt anyone to have some fun," she said knowingly.

"Fun leads to relationships," Charly reminded her friends. "I can't do a relationship. Not even a casual one. I haven't even dealt with my last one. Shouldn't I at least talk to Marcel before I end up in someone else's bed?"

Aubrey shrugged. "Nothing wrong with rebound."

"When you're emotionally put together," Charly said. "Which I am definitely not." The anger of Marcel's betrayal burned within her. Her heart still bled. "I don't want to make my life more complicated than it already is."

"That's fair," Willow said.

Charly grabbed one of the muffins for the road and her to-go cup and said, "All right, I'm doing this. Wish me luck."

Willow chuckled. "You can do it!"

"Good luck," Aubrey said, and as Charly headed down the hallway, she heard Aubrey add, "She's totally going to sleep with him."

"My bets on that too," Willow said with a laugh.

Charly sighed...*again*. She pushed those thoughts aside and smiled in pride at the house around her. They'd made their home truly theirs. After they moved in, they'd pooled together all their money and hired a construction company to strip the walls, floors, crown molding, and window and door trim down to the core before refinishing everything in red mahogany. The peeling wallpaper was gone, with most of the walls now painted white in various shades bringing character to each room. The old house looked as if it was back in its prime with the same character that Charly had fallen in love with.

A part of her thought that's what she had done with the bar. But now she wondered if she'd gone too far and changed it too much.

Ignoring Willow and Aubrey still chatting in the kitchen, she hurried out the front door and got into her four-door sedan. She typed Jaxon's address into Google Maps that he texted her last night, and was on the road a moment later, scarfing down her muffin. The road was quiet and peaceful and everything at one time in her life she would've hated. She'd always loved the city, the adventure, the excitement, people, the noise even, but now she couldn't find love in any of that anymore. It all reminded her of a life she wanted to forget and the pain she refused to face.

Twenty minutes later, the feminine voice indicated through the car's speakers that she had arrived. Yet again, the view stole the very air from her lungs.

The soft yellow light of the summer morning filtered through one of the old oak trees atop the hill. Charly drove up the driveway, taking in the shimmering vision of the horse ranch laid out before her. The fields were lush and verdant, the tall grasses rippling in the gentle breeze. The outbuildings, mostly faded red, and white barns, were clustered around the main house, and there were several smaller buildings scattered around them. At the far end of the field, she could make out a pasture filled with horses, each one more beautiful than the last.

As she pulled up to the log house, parking next to a truck, the front door opened, and Jaxon came out on the porch. She swallowed deeply, pushing the rising heat in her core far...*far*...down. Leaning against the porch's railing, he wore a white T-shirt, worn blue jeans and scuffed-up cowboy boots. And goddamn did he fill out his jeans close to a perfection that no man should be able to do.

Worst of all, seeing that knowing smirk on his face that declared he knew she liked what she saw made her want to bleach her eyes out for how they betrayed her.

After she stepped out, shutting the car's door behind her, his heated gaze raked over her from head to toe.

When his eyes met hers again, he grinned. "Looking like a cowboy."

She refused to squirm under his potent stare, staying tall and firm. "Figured wearing this was better than high heels."

His low chuckle brushed delicately across her. "Yeah, probably a wise decision." He came down the rest of the steps, and surprising her, he leaned in and kissed her cheek.

She attempted to fight leaning into him, and she failed miserably. The moment his lips met her skin, the memory of him kissing his way down her neck and his low groans squeezed her thighs tight for the friction. The pleasure he had offered, making her lose her mind, all came back to her, prickling goose bumps across her skin.

No!

She clamped down on those thoughts, pulling away. She

needed to get over one heartbreak before letting anything happen again.

His red flags, Charly. All the red flags!

"All right," she said, purposely taking a full step back, "what's exactly the plan here?"

He tracked her movement and grinned. "I suggest you let the girls know you'll be here for four days, so they'll have to cover you."

"Four days?" she blessedly managed not to gasp. "We never agreed to that. I'm here for today, that's it."

He watched her closely then offered an easy shrug. "If you really want to see what life in Timber Falls is all about then you're going to have to experience what cowboys do. You won't get the full understanding from being here for a day." He cocked his head, arching a brow. "Unless learning about the people of Timber Falls isn't really that important to you."

Oh, the jerk. "You know it's important. I'll decide if I need more than one day here."

His mouth twitched, his eyes all but laughing at her as he waved out. "As you wish." She stepped into stride with him as they headed toward the red barn and he continued, "We've got a busy four days coming up at the ranch, but they're some of the most important."

"Why?" she asked, glancing around the farm seeing a few farmhands working about, pushing wheel barrels and walking horses to the fields.

He shoved his hands into his pockets. "We're doing our yearly roundup and auction. That consists of moving the two-year-old horses from their field and bringing them up to the pastures here. We sort them then decide which ones stay for training. Those get put into another pasture, and the others go into the paddock there." He pointed ahead of him, before addressing her again. "We hold a big event here where people from all over North America come to purchase one of our horses."

"What exactly is the big event?" she asked.

"We host an auction with a catered meal with Big Boy's barbeque, and we enjoy some horses."

She kept trying to see where she fit in. "What exactly am I going to do in all of this?"

"Today we're doing a couple things. First, I'm going to show you around the ranch and introduce you to every-body here. If you got any questions for any of the cowboys about what they'd like to see at the bar, or what they think is missing, feel free to ask them. There's a good group of people working here."

"Okay." *Good.* She needed to get her answers and get out before she had another mental breakdown and jumped the hot sex in jeans next to her.

He tilted his head. "Have you ever ridden a horse before?"

She nodded. "A couple times, but I'm not experienced. I've mostly gone out on the trail rides on vacations and things like that."

"A little experience is better than nothing," he said. "I figured today we could work with giving you a riding lesson. And then after that, you'll need to go home and pack a bag for your stay here."

Her brows rose and she cursed the heat brimming inside at the inappropriate thoughts filling her mind. "Why do I have to stay here?"

Like he was plucking those thoughts right out of her mind, he smirked. "We head out at sunrise tomorrow and ride out to the horses. It's a day's ride out and it's a day right back, so we'll be camping out."

"Like in a tent?" she asked.

"No tent," he said. "Under the stars."

She sighed, imagining the bugs that would crawl over her. "We couldn't make an exception for one little tent?"

Again, a single brow lifted. "You did say you want to understand our way of life, right?"

"Yeah, I said that." She began regretting saying that though.

"There's no better way to understand life in Timber Falls then coming out with us on the roundup and experiencing what we do." A pause. Then he took a step forward, closing the distance between them. "Besides…" His voice lowered into a husky tone, seeping heady heat into her entire body. "It gives a little more time for you to get to know me."

She watched him carefully, looking for some trick, some play she was missing. She simply didn't see one, and that was the most dangerous thing of all. "You can stop this you know."

He took another step forward, bringing all that strength close. "Stop what?"

"Whatever happened before is out of my system," she said firmly. "It was a weak moment on my part that will never happen again."

His mouth twitched. "You're trying to tell me that with this kind of chemistry between us, you'll be able to sleep next to me and not want to kiss the hell out of me."

"That's exactly what I'm telling you," she said, adamant.

He chuckled, low and deep. "Yeah, we'll see about that, Kitten." When she frowned at the nickname, he tapped her nose. "All claws, hisses and bites, but exceptionally cute." Before she could react, he closed the rest of the distance, only centimeters between them now. She felt his breath on her lips, making her melt into her boots. "Gotta say, though, my favorite is when you're purring beneath me."

Her breath hitched, stealing all logical thoughts from her brain.

He smirked, gestured ahead of him. "Come on, Kitten, let me show you around."

Somehow, she remembered how to make her legs work and she followed, reminding herself of one very important fact—*He is the devil!*

As Jaxon stepped out of the rustic wooden barn after having spent the last hour showing Charly around the ranch, beams of sunlight spread across the area, bathing it in a gentle, golden glow. His gaze wandered across the sprawling expanse of lush grasses speckled with wildflowers that danced in the breeze. The horses munched happily on grass, their coats shining brightly in the sun. He looked over at Charly and smiled fondly at her content expression. Surprisingly enough, she seemed right at home despite being a city girl.

Jaxon led Charly toward a cowboy waiting by the sand ring. "This is Charly," Jaxon said as they drew nearer. "Decker, this is Charly."

Decker gave her a thorough glance over and smiled, crinkling his dark eyes at the corners and showing off pearly white teeth. He held on to the reins attached to Thunder, their ranch's most docile horse. Thunder had once been Jaxon's father's prize possession, a beloved horse that knew and loved his job. Jaxon stared into the horse's dark eyes and his chest softened, feeling like his father was there watching over the ranch.

Decker tipped his black cowboy hat. "Well, hello there, Charly." He beamed with too much enthusiasm for Jaxon's taste.

Jaxon sighed heavily as thoughts of having all these men working on his ranch ran through his head yet again. He was proud to have such a loyal and hardworking team of men and women working on his ranch—until Charly arrived. He couldn't help the rush of jealousy that filled him when the men would look in her direction. He knew he had no right to be possessive, but he couldn't bear the thought of anyone else getting too close to her during her stay at the ranch. He wanted to get to know her better himself.

He cleared his throat, drawing Decker's attention to him and prompting the man to stop smiling so widely.

In a more serious tone, Decker asked, "So I hear you took over the bar?"

Charly nodded. "Me and some of my friends," she replied.

"That's why she's here," Jaxon quickly added. "To learn more about life in town to help the locals feel more welcome at the bar."

Decker gave her an inquisitive look. "At your bar that caters to heartbroken out-of-towners?"

Charly let out a deep sigh. "Is that what people are saying?"

"Well ma'am it is," Decker stated, rubbing the back of his neck sheepishly. "Sorry if that's not what you wanted to hear."

She fixed her gaze on him intently, a frown marring her features. "Thank you for telling me. I appreciate your honesty, and that is why I'm here. We want to make everyone feel welcome in the bar. And we're not just creating a safe space for heartbroken out-of-towners, it's to celebrate achievements too. For everyone. Most importantly, for the people in town."

Growing curious, Jaxon asked, "Would you throw a party for a man going through a breakup?"

She glanced over at him briefly before nodding. "Of course, if they wanted one." Peering at him closely she muttered suspiciously, "Why, Jaxon? Has someone broken your heart recently?" She paused and grinned, all sass. "Oh, right, you don't do relationships."

Decker coughed lightly to hide his amused laughter.

Jaxon let the dig roll off him. She thought he was scum—maybe even worse than scum. It got right under his skin. *She* got right under his skin. "Nah, no recent breakups." He edged closer to her, her cheeks flushing with color at his nearness. "I never said that I don't do relationships, Charly," he murmured softly. His words had the desired effect as her breath caught in her throat and heat filled her gaze. He could feel the tension between them too, his cock hardening to respond to it. He grinned, before taking the reins from Decker's hand, saying to him, "Thanks. We won't be too long."

"I'll be here when you're done," Decker said. He tipped his hat to Charly and added, "Enjoy your ride."

"Thanks, Decker," she said with a smile. "It was nice to meet you."

Decker smiled again, only this time with less eagerness than before.

Jaxon took in her warm smile with a glimmer of hope that it contained nothing more than friendliness. The ladies liked Decker.

As soon as the thought crossed his mind, Jaxon shook his head at himself. When had he become...*jealous*?

"You've got a really nice group working here, don't you?" Charly asked, drawing him away from his thoughts.

He nodded, opening the gate and heading into the sand ring. "We've got good people here in Timber Falls."

But she disagreed, shaking her head and commenting, "Every cowboy I've met before today has been cranky."

Raising an eyebrow at her, he leaned closer and questioned jokingly, "Even this cowboy?"

"You have your moments." She laughed and glanced away ahead of her.

Chuckling softly—something he seemed to do a lot with her around—he couldn't take his eyes off her as she headed through the gate, and he and Thunder followed. He tried to pinpoint what it was about Charly that captivated him. She was a challenge, certainly, but it wasn't about a game with her. There was something...*there*. Something that made him want to wrap himself around the feeling she stirred in him and keep it and savor its warmth.

As they continued through the sand ring, Jaxon took in the gorgeous day on the ranch. The bright blue sky was clear, the sun was bright, warming the earth and everything on it. The air tasted of dry, unforgiving heat, and while he did miss the bar, spending his days outdoors again brought an unexpected comfort, making him feel like his father was always nearby.

"Is that Gunner and Eli?" she asked, dragging his gaze to her.

He followed where she was looking, spotting them farther down the sand ring, riding horses. "Yeah, they both work for me."

"Have they always?" she asked.

"Growing up, they worked on the ranch during the summers and on the weekends for my dad, just like I did. But both only recently came back home. Gunner, a year ago, after living in Nashville. He's a singer in a country music band. His last album didn't do so well, so he's now taking time off from touring to write new music. As for Eli, he came back six months ago, but his story is a bit complicated. I'll tell you about it another time."

Charly watched him closely, but let it go with a slow nod.

When they finally reached the center of the sand ring, Eli and Gunner glanced their way and then trotted over on their mounts.

Gunner grinned at Charly. "Don't look so scared. Thunder will take good care of you."

"I'm not scared, but he better not hurt me," Charly said to not only Jaxon but Thunder too.

The horse snorted, as if he understood, and Jaxon let out a laugh. He'd never met a woman like Charly either.

"I would never put you up on his back if I thought you'd get hurt," Jaxon told her, then gestured for her to move forward. As she stepped closer to Thunder, Jaxon moved in behind her. He placed his hands on her waist and felt the residual trembles that ran through her body. Heat enveloped him as he recalled the way those tremors melted away into soft moans beneath his fingertips. He bit back a groan as his cock went from semihard to steel instantly, and he fought against drawing her closer.

He slid his hand down her left arm and took her hand, setting one hand on the horse's mane and the other he placed on the back of the saddle. Stepping even closer, he ran his hand down her thigh. "All right, give me your leg," he murmured. "Bend your knee and do a little hop when I count three to help hoist you up." On his count, she hopped, and he lifted her leg over the saddle.

Once she settled into the tack, he took a step back and watched as she held the reins in her left hand properly, confirming that she'd ridden a few times before. "Thunder knows his job," he said, tucking his hands into his pockets. "All you need to do is be comfortable in the saddle and if you feel unsteady, grab onto the horn and hold on tight. Thunder will never go too fast or throw you off."

"Okay," she said with a soft nod. She stroked Thunder's neck. "We're going to get along just fine, then."

Jaxon agreed with a nod. "Give him a nudge with your legs to walk forward," he said.

She did as he instructed, and Thunder moved forward calmly.

When they were out of hearing distance, Eli asked, "Is feeling someone up a new way to offer a leg-up?"

Gunner barked a laugh, but Jaxon didn't reply. Instead, he kept walking closer to Charly. "A squeeze of your legs will get him into a trot."

Again, she followed his instructions without hesitating and gave Thunder a light squeeze of her ankles.

"Good," he called after she trotted a little while. "Take hold of the horn and squeeze again to get him to lope."

Thunder began loping around the ring, and Charly sat easily on him while they smoothly transitioned between each gait, until she came back to a walk.

When she turned Thunder and headed back toward him, Charly's face was split into an enormous grin as she patted Thunder's neck affectionately.

"See? Nothing to worry about," Jaxon said with a smile. "You did great, and you'll do just fine on the roundup."

"Thanks," she said, continuing to stroke Thunder's neck as the horse stopped in front of him. "You're right, he's a very good boy."

Jaxon took hold of Thunder's reins, never feeling so jealous of a horse before. He craved for her hand to be traveling over him.

Ignoring what Eli and Gunner had said, he stepped up to help her off the horse, holding her by the waist as she dismounted. She slid down his body, and he fought back a moan, but didn't stop her from feeling his erection. He wasn't totally convinced she hadn't done that on purpose, but a quick look into her face and her expression revealed nothing.

Beginning to feel like he was punishing himself by having her there, Jaxon whistled, and Decker came jogging over. He hopped over the fence, taking the reins from Jaxon.

Decker winked at Charly. "Well done!"

"Thanks." She beamed.

Jaxon watched the interaction with a scowl. Decker took one look at him, and promptly turned away, leading the horse back into the barn to take off its tack, though his shoulders shook with silent laughter.

Eli coughed, obviously failing to hide his laughter.

Jaxon glanced back toward his friends, both Eli and Gunner were smirking at him. He needed to get a hold of himself. This woman was turning him upside down.

"So now what?" she asked, her eyes keen with excitement.

He ran a hand across the back of his neck, letting the tension fall away. "We're going downtown."

She followed him out of the sand ring, saying goodbye to Eli and Gunner as they left. "Why?"

"A real cowboy isn't a cowboy without wearing proper boots and a hat."

"It's Sunday," she said. "Nothing is open."

"The owner owes me a favor, and you need the right attire for the long ride."

She snorted and seemed reluctant to continue, but eventually lifted her head high as she spoke again. "Sorry, but whatever I'm wearing is all I can use right now. This is about as country as I can get with my clothes, and we put all our money into the bar."

He respected that she had invested everything in making her dream come true. It brought relief knowing she was doing what she could do to make sure his bar didn't sink. "The ranch provides every cowboy what they need. It won't cost you anything."

She laughed out loud in obvious disbelief. "But I'm not really a cowboy."

He grinned at her words. "Tomorrow, you will be."

Nine

Just before dinner, Charly returned home, exhausted from the day at the ranch, carrying two boxes in her arms. She found Willow sitting comfortably on the gray-colored plush sofa and Aubrey was tucked away in a brown leather arm-chair. The walls were decorated with vintage photographs and paintings they had picked up at the farmer's market. Gentle rays of sunshine from the setting sun spilled through the lacy window curtains creating a welcoming atmosphere by brightening up the wooden beams and stone fireplace.

"What's that?" Willow asked as Charly kicked the door shut behind her.

"Cowboy boots and a hat," Charly answered, laughing as they gawked at her. "Yes, I know. Hilarious. But Jaxon said its proper attire for the roundup we're doing tomorrow."

"What's a roundup?" Aubrey asked, hurrying from her spot on the love seat to take one of the boxes out of her arms. She placed it onto the entryway table and opened the lid revealing beautiful dark brown boots with teal embroidery. "Damn, these are gorgeous."

"I know." Charly set the other box next to the boots, which held a tan cowboy hat. "I can't wait to pair both with jeans and a white button-down."

"Where did you get these?" Willow asked, coming closer.

"Jaxon took me to a place downtown." Charly offered Willow the hat. "The owner owed him a favor so he came in. I tried to pay for everything, but Jaxon refused, and said it was the ranch's uniform."

"Pretty nice uniforms." Willow tried on the hat and glanced in the mirror above the table saying, "Hells yeah, stunning."

"About the roundup?" Audrey asked again.

"Oh, right," Charly said, taking a seat on the second to last step of the staircase. Her feet hurt. Her body ached. She'd only walked around the ranch, and had a short ride, and found it exhausting. She couldn't imagine a whole day's worth of work and riding there. "Jaxon has asked me to stay at the ranch for the next few days. They're riding out to round up some of the horses to bring them back for an auction, and he wants me to immerse myself in that." Willow set the hat back in the box as Charly added, "I know this will put you two out since I won't be at the bar, but I think it's important. I was told today that the word on the street is our place is for heartbroken out-of-towners only."

"Ouch," Aubrey said. "Definitely not what we were going for."

Willow agreed with a nod. "We can handle the bar just fine. You're right. It *is* important. We want everyone in town to feel welcome. We need to learn more about the people here. I'll talk to Betty too—maybe she has some good ideas."

"That's a great idea," Charly agreed.

Aubrey set the boots on the floor near the front door. "Not trying to be a Debbie Downer, but you think you're up for spending a night in the wilderness?"

Charly laughed and shrugged. "No, but there isn't a chance in hell that I'm going to let any of those cowboys see how little I want to be there. I'll just use an obscene amount of bug spray and hope it keeps every single creepy crawler off me."

Laughter filled the foyer, a sound that was becoming more and more frequent in the house lately, filling Charly's chest with warmth. They'd lived in Michigan, in California, and now in Montana together, and this home was starting to feel more comfortable and less unfamiliar.

Aubrey finally gestured toward the living room. "I grabbed us a pizza. Are you hungry?"

"Starving," Charly replied.

The aroma of hot bread, grease and grilled meat filled her senses as she settled onto the couch next to Willow. Her tummy grumbled in delight at the sight of Carl's pizza logo emblazoned on the box, probably one of the only places open on Sunday. She had tried numerous pizzerias in Phoenix, yet none compared to the flavor of Carl's recipe.

"So," Aubrey began, dropping down onto the love seat across from the couch, "What have you learned so far about being at the ranch?"

Charly took a bite from her pizza before answering. "To be honest it was all quite surprising."

Willow grabbed another slice of pizza from the box. "Why?"

"I think we can all agree that the cowboys we've encountered around here have been grouchy," Charly explained. "But back at the ranch they were all polite, hardworking and decent people."

Willow wiped her mouth clean with a napkin, glancing between them both. "That's a good thing, isn't it?"

"I suppose," Charly said slowly, trying to pull her thoughts together. "It just wasn't what I was expecting. In my mind, I thought I'd arrive there and meet a bunch of jerks that would never be satisfied with any kind of new business venture, especially one run by women and who had taken over the bar of their boss. But I liked them which makes me feel a bit awful for taking away their beloved western bar and replacing it with a cocktail bar."

Aubrey raised an eyebrow. "Was that said today?"

Charly nodded. "I told a few of them that said so that was never our intention, and that we're more about celebrating accomplishments and wanted everyone to feel welcome. However, I didn't really get the feeling that they believed me."

Willow cocked her head, looking sheepish through her lashes. "We did kind of change everything about the bar."

"We did," Charly agreed, "but it's quite possible that they were being on their best behavior due to Jaxon's presence because he is the boss."

"That could be true," Aubrey said with a nod. "All right, so here's what you missed at the bar."

Charly savored every bite of her pizza, listening as her friends updated her on the deliveries and three new parties that had been scheduled for women who lived out of the area. One to celebrate a promotion. Another for a cancer survivor. And one other for a "swap party," where everyone swapped a few items of clothing they had brought with them.

"That's brilliant!" she commented.

Willow grinned, brushing crumbs from her lips with a napkin. "The ideas have been coming thick and fast recently."

"So, what else have you thought up?" Charly asked.

"How about *Bachelorette* screenings every week? Or a *Sex in the City* rewatch? Book releases? Tattoo reveal parties that we set up with the local tattoo shop? Those are just some of the events I've been thinking about," Willow replied.

"Yes! Yes! Yes!" Charly said happily. "That all sounds great, Willow."

At Willow's beaming face filled with pride, Charly felt

warmth in her chest. She wanted their bar to feel like a community where friends could gather, where people were celebrated and enjoyed. Now she just needed to get the locals to feel that way too. She stuffed the last piece of bread into her mouth and fell back onto the couch with a sigh. "I'm so full." She chuckled.

"That only means you ate the perfect amount." Willow grinned.

Right then, Charly's cell phone started ringing back in her purse in the foyer. Her heart jumped into her throat, before she stuffed *that* feeling away. Her excitement totally wasn't over a certain cowboy. Nope, not about Jaxon at all.

She scurried to the foyer and grabbed her cell from her purse. Her heart sank at who was calling.

"It's Marcel," she informed the girls.

Aubrey quirked an eyebrow. "I don't understand guys like him at all. Why do they realize what they have after screwing up?"

"No clue," uttered Charly as she stared at her phone. His calls would never end unless she acted. She wasn't sure if it was from her off-the-charts hot night with Jaxon that she was still trying to forget about. Or maybe even that she and the girls were doing better now—they were making their way out of the dark abyss of their sadness—but she knew she needed to move on from Marcel. She couldn't help but wonder if her mom was right—she needed to finally face this head-on.

Making up her mind, she responded to the phone call. "Hello."

"Charly," Marcel whispered in his low voice that once caused her skin to prickle with goose bumps.

She paused for a moment, taking in his heavy breathing.

"Thank you for picking up," he said, after a long moment.

She stayed locked on her friends wide eyes as she asked, "Why do you keep calling me, Marcel?"

"I'm worried about you..." he said and then hesitated before snorting. "Shit. I know how messed up that must sound considering what I did to you...but I—"

"You don't have to feel concerned about me," she stated. For the first time, she chose to keep her boiling anger to herself. "I'm doing great."

"How can you be?" he argued back. "You've abandoned everything and moved to the middle of nowhere. I am responsible for this. I robbed your life away from you."

She closed her eyes, allowing herself to drift into a peaceful darkness and sighed deeply. "I shouldn't have left without talking to you and settling all this. Maybe it was wrong of me or maybe understandable given all that occurred... but all I know is that I have to move on...and I need to do that now."

A long pause filled the phone line before he replied, "You do deserve that. I will never be able to forgive myself for hurting you...for what you witnessed..."

It dawned on her that while she would usually come out

with some cruel comment meant to hurt him, she couldn't find those harsh words now. "It's time to move on, Marcel. Please don't call again," she said, opening her eyes to her friends. Both were looking back at her warmly and lovingly. "I've created a new life for myself. One that makes me happy. If my mother tries to talk to you again, tell her what I've said."

He paused. Longer this time. Then he said softly, "You don't want me to explain why I did what I did? You don't need a reason?"

Nothing he said would change anything. "No, Marcel, I don't."

His voice cracked. "If that's what you want, I'll leave you alone then."

She felt her breaking heart shudder as the pain of what-could-have-been swept through her entire being. "Goodbye, Marcel."

"Goodbye, Charly."

She ended the call, opened his contact information and blocked his number. "Blocked. Done and done!"

Aubrey and Willow leaped off the couch and gave Charly a tight hug, like they'd been waiting for weeks for her to make that decision. And maybe they had.

"This is a good thing," said Willow, squeezing Charly hard. "Now you can put that asshole behind you."

"Definitely," chorused Aubrey.

And yet, a small part of her heart was fractured at the thought of not caring if Marcel contacted her again or knowing what he was doing with his life. She had once planned an entire future with him. Although the larger part of her heart would never take him back, there was a tiny bit that cherished the dream she thought they'd share together.

It hurt to let that dream die.

"Let's go," Charly said, stepping out of their arms.

"Where?" Aubrey inquired.

She sauntered toward the stairs, each one creaking beneath her bare feet. "You need to help me pack. I have to wake up at a stupid time tomorrow morning to head out with the cowboys. When we got back at the ranch, Jaxon suggested I stay in his guest room tonight to make sure I'm not late in the morning."

Aubrey snorted. "Sure."

Willow giggled.

"It isn't like that," Charly argued as she entered her bedroom. The vintage four-poster bed was the focal point in the room, its aged wooden frame exuding character and warmth. A soft, pastel-colored rug cushioned the hardwood floor beneath it. She got out her carry-on suitcase from the small closet, and placed it on the bed. "What happened between us was a one-time deal. I have no intention of getting involved with a guy with major commitment issues. Besides, I'm sleeping outside with a bunch of cowboys on the roundup—not exactly romantic."

"I disagree," Aubrey remarked, waggling her eyebrows. "I'm sure there are romance books about a lady with a bunch of cowboys, and they're probably very steamy."

Charly tossed a pillow at Aubrey who caught it and laughed. "Then you should go if it sounds so tempting."

Willow just shook her head at them and leaned against the dresser, grinning.

"Anyways," Charly drawled, changing the subject, giving Aubrey a *look*. "I found out something today," she announced to Willow and Aubrey as she put some jeans in her bag.

"Oh?" Aubrey said, dropping onto the bed.

"Gunner, Jaxon's friend, is a country singer," Charly informed them.

Willow's eyes widened. "Really?"

"YouTube him," Charly suggested, pulling out a couple long T-shirts that she used as pajamas, as well as a pair of tight shorts since she didn't want to give the cowboys any ideas when she slept out with them. "See what you can find out about him."

Willow grabbed her phone from her back pocket and began typing and soon the sound of an alluring masculine voice filled the room.

"Is that him?" Charly asked.

Willow nodded as she read through an article on her phone. "It says here that his last album didn't do so well on the charts, but his one before went platinum."

Charly asked, "So, he's famous then?"

"Looks like it," Willow replied. "He has 1.5 million followers on Instagram."

"Impressive," Charly remarked.

Willow showed them photos from past concerts in stadiums as well as recent shots of him with the ranch and cowboys.

"Why is he at the ranch now?" Aubrey asked Charly. "He's not singing anymore?"

She shrugged. "Jaxon said that he came home for a break and to work on some new music."

"What about Eli?" asked Willow curiously. "What's his story?"

"I'm not quite sure about him," Charly responded, adding panties to her bag. Even put in plain cottons ones to remind herself the next days were not about sexiness. "Jaxon said Eli's story was a little more complicated and he'd tell me later."

"Sounds mysterious," Aubrey said.

Charly had been thinking this same thought all day long. "Honestly, I have a feeling there's something rather mysterious about all three of those cowboys." Before her thoughts ran away with her, she added firmly, "Which doesn't matter, because the only reason I'm there is to find out how to make the locals at the bar happy and to learn more about life here in Timber Falls."

Aubrey rolled her eyes. "Sure, Charly, keep telling yourself that."

"I will," she told Aubrey, and herself.

Jaxon was lounging on the porch railing in a wooden chair with his ankles resting on the railing as Charly drove up with a trail of dust bellowing behind her car. The sun had just begun to set, and the sky was glowing pink, promising a beautiful day to come tomorrow. Last year's roundup had taken place during a torrential downpour and he knew Charly couldn't have endured it. Even he and the ranch's cowboys had been miserable and barely made it through.

Charly parked her car next to his truck and got out, retrieving her suitcase from the back seat.

"Are you all set?" he asked, jumping up and trotting down the steps to take her bag from her.

"Yep, I'm good." She looked around the ranch before focusing on him again, then walked up the porch steps. "Where has everyone else gone?"

"Home for the night," he said. He let his gaze roam over her—she was just so damn beautiful. "It's only you and me now, Kitten. Think you can handle that without ravishing me?"

She laughed softly, raising her chin. "Please. I can restrain myself. You don't have to worry about that."

He smiled at her, and loved when her focus went to his lips. Did she remember how hot their kissing had been too? How mind-blowing it had been to touch her? "Do you want something to drink? A beer?"

"Sure, why not," she replied.

He headed inside the house, leaving her bag just inside the door, and grabbed her a beer from the fridge. He cracked it open on his way back outside and handed it to her as she sat in the chair next to him.

"Thank you," she said after taking a long sip from the bottle. "Is no one else living on this property?"

"Just me," he answered with a tilt of his head. "You seem surprised by that?"

"I guess I am a little bit," she said. "I thought all cowboys on ranches lived on them too, just like they do in movies or TV shows."

He chuckled. "Nothing's like it is on TV."

"I guess that's true," she said, tearing her gaze away to look out at the view around her.

He knew why she was so mesmerized by the horses grazing in the paddocks. There was a certain peace here that simply couldn't be found anywhere else. "My dad believed that those who worked for him deserved a place of their own—somewhere that belonged to only them, a *home*. He said it made his cowboys happier people, and I think he was right."

He couldn't quite tell what she was thinking when she met his gaze again, and asked, "So, your father really took good care of his employees then, huh?"

"Always did." He picked up his beer bottle from the porch floor and held it between two fingers.

Part of him felt like he shouldn't touch on her past life, but the other part of him wanted to unravel all her secrets. "Did your ex run your business like that?"

She finished her sip of her beer and stared back out at the horses. "No, Marcel didn't have that same view. He believed every worker was replaceable." She gave a dry laugh before shaking her head sadly. "Including his fiancée."

"His loss," Jaxon said immediately. He couldn't imagine having Charly as his and replacing her. He'd only known her for a short time, and he couldn't take his eyes off her.

This time, when she met his gaze, she smiled warmly. "Definitely."

A comfortable silence ensued as she studied the rosy sky and sighed deeply, a soft sound releasing every worry and hardship. Jaxon understood. Life could carry a heavy burden at times. And somehow the open fresh air, and the peace at the ranch could quiet those burdens.

"So, after the cowboys leave here, they go home?" she asked, breaking the silence.

"They go to the bar," he replied before taking another swig of his beer. "Then they go home."

"Do they do that every day?"

He knew why she was asking, and this was part of their deal with her being there. With that in mind, he thought of his regular customers when he owned the bar and his cowboys and answered her, "As you likely saw today, and will continue to see in the coming days, Timber Falls' towns-folk work very hard. They deserve a moment for fun now and then, so they look for somewhere to go to blow off steam—that used to be my bar."

She paused and regarded him with curiosity. "Until we took over?"

"It's not a dig," he said, reading the fire burning in her

gaze. "I'm just pointing out that there wasn't any other place around here to socialize until I owned the bar."

Charly mulled over his words, nodding slowly in understanding. "Thank you for answering. It's something to consider."

"Anything you want to know, Charly, just ask," he said, leaning back in his chair. Which reminded him she had asked an earlier question he had yet to answer about Eli. After all, he knew she was seeing more of him soon enough, and Eli always gave his blessing to talk about what happened in his past. "You asked me earlier about Eli," he said. "Normally, I wouldn't say anything and let you talk to Eli himself, but I've seen others feel uncomfortable when it comes up randomly."

"Okay," she drawled, curiosity brimming in her eyes.

He took another sip of his beer before setting it down again. "His younger sister was murdered, and that's why he moved back to town."

Charly's eyes widened in shock, and she nearly choked on her drink. "Murdered? What happened?"

The memory of the violent crime still felt fresh in his mind, even though months had passed since it happened. "She was killed while Eli was on the Professional Rodeo circuit."

Her nose scrunched up. "Sorry, what is the rodeo circuit?"

"He's a professional bull rider, and a promising one at that." It tore Jaxon apart that Eli had to walk away from his dreams. It was one thing he wished they didn't have in common. "For eight months, no one knew that Eli's little sister, Miranda, was being abused by her boyfriend. Unfortunately, it was too late by the time anyone found out. Her boyfriend had killed her when she tried to break up with him."

Charly held a hand to her chest, shaking her head as she said, "That's tragic."

"Very," Jaxon replied. "He's in jail. Hopefully for the rest of his life." He watched her for a moment, sensing something on her mind. "What is it?"

"Willow's ex-boyfriend was abusive," Charly murmured, her voice full of emotion.

"Willow?" he asked in surprise. "Was she hurt?"

"I know, it's hard to believe," Charly said. "How anyone could raise a hand against someone as sweet as Willow? But I think that's why she was so vulnerable with him. She had it in her head that she wanted to help him." She hesitated, clearly gathering her emotions before adding, "He put her in the hospital and gave her thirteen stitches, so yeah, it was bad."

He'd noticed the scar on her cheekbone when he'd first met her, but figured it was a childhood injury or a car accident. "Where's this guy now?" Jaxon asked.

"In jail," Charly answered grimly. "Where I hope he stays for a very long time."

"No kidding," Jaxon agreed as one of the horses neighed off in the distance. "Is that one of the reasons why you all moved here?" He couldn't help but wonder what would bring a bunch of city girls to a rustic town in Montana.

"Partially," she said softly. "But it's safe to say we were all running away from something when we got on that plane for Timber Falls." Taking a long sip from her beer, she eventually added, "I'm just so relieved Willow isn't with him anymore and is here safe and sound."

"I couldn't agree with you more," Jaxon said with a nod. "Miranda's murder destroyed Eli. He's never been quite the same since. And she lost her beautiful vibrant life. So much was stolen from them."

"What a tragedy."

"It is, so please be mindful of discussing anything related to this on the roundup to Eli."

She watched him closely for a moment, with an unreadable expression. "Are you protecting him?"

"Not protecting," he countered. "But if I can save him from pain, I will."

He couldn't figure out her thoughts—she was very good at locking down her expression—but for a moment her expression softened, and he got the feeling that she liked his answer.

Good. Maybe she'd stop seeing him as a man full of red flags. He wanted her to see *him*. The real him, and the thought wasn't lost on him that he couldn't recall a time he'd ever wanted that before.

The minutes passed easily as they chatted while finishing their drinks, and he felt comfort in her presence. He liked hearing about her parents in Ann Arbor, how her dad was supportive of her decision to break away from her awful former fiancé, but her mother was having a harder time with the split. He also found out about her younger sister, Collette, who was studying to be a lawyer in the United Kingdom. The more she spoke, the more he knew she was smart, seemed to love her family, regardless if they weren't perfect, and she seemed to value the relationships in her life.

When the sun finally set, and darkness settled in, he proceeded to take the empty bottles into the house and then carried her suitcase down the hall. "This will be your room for tonight," he said. The room was his childhood bedroom, only big enough for a queen-sized bed made of reclaimed barn wood, adorned with a patchwork quilt, and a small bedside table. He put her bag on the bed and motioning at the adjacent doorway. "There's a bathroom with a shower inside, towels are in the cabinets next to it."

"Thanks," she replied.

He nodded before going to the door to the hallway, stopping in its frame and crossing his arms as he studied her intently. He couldn't help but smile as she began to blush slightly.

Excellent. That meant that he wasn't the only one thinking of how they could spend their time together tonight.

He quirked an eyebrow at her. "Anything else I can do for you, Charly?" He'd asked the question, almost daring her to take him up on it.

She licked her lips and bit down on the bottom one,

glancing at him like she was one step away from jumping into his arms and climbing up his body. "Stop that, Kitten," he murmured.

"Stop what?" she asked in a husky voice.

He closed the gap between them until he could feel the white-hot sparks of electricity crackling around them. "Eating me up with your eyes."

A flicker of annoyance shone in those seductive eyes as she took a step back and lifted her chin. "Don't think so highly of yourself," she stated coldly. "That's *not* what I'm doing."

He gave her a playful smirk. "Ah, there are those claws I like so much." Returning to the hallway, he turned back to her. "Good night, Charly. Set your alarm for five a.m. for grub."

Charly huffed out an exasperated breath and shut the door in his face. "Good night, Jaxon."

She was going to lose this fight. He knew it. He suspected she knew it too.

His laughter echoed down the hallway as he headed off toward his bedroom, knowing full well he wouldn't be getting any sleep with the fiery woman nearby.

Ten

It should be against the law to wake up at five in the morning, Charly thought as she sat at the carved wooden island and managed to stuff down the eggs, bacon and toast that Jaxon had made. Sexy as hell, and the man could cook, she was starting to think Montana men were made of different stuff.

Better stuff.

He had obviously woken up earlier than her, and he was bright-eyed with a big smile on his face the moment she entered the kitchen. She'd glared at him just because of it. How was anyone that happy before the sun rose?

By her second cup of coffee, she was less of a monster and more of a human being and took in her surroundings better.

Jaxon's childhood home spoke of family with photographs from the ranch throughout the years. The walls of the kitchen were constructed from solid logs, and the cupboards were built with aged pine and decorated with iron handles. In the corner of the room, a farmhouse table was placed in front of the window with a collection of mismatched wooden chairs hugging it.

Her attention drifted to the wall, where a black-and-white photograph hung of a man on a horse. "Who's that?" she asked.

Jaxon finished putting his plate into the dishwasher and then followed her gaze. "That's my grandfather on my father's side. He was a fantastic horseman. Taught my father everything he knew."

"Which he then taught you?" she asked.

"That's right," he agreed.

She glanced to the other photograph on the table. "Is that your mom and dad?"

Jaxon grabbed the picture, glancing at the photo behind the glass. "Yeah, this is my parents' wedding day." He turned the frame to her. "Not a bad lookin' couple, huh?"

"Your mother was beautiful," she said in agreement.

He nodded. "Yeah, she was." But beneath his tough exterior she saw the longing there. He obviously missed his family. Her heart squeezed for him. Even if her mother could drive her batty sometimes by loving her a little too much, she couldn't imagine not having her parents.

She rose and put her mug in the dishwasher, as Jaxon said, "Boot up, Kitten, I'll see you out there." He winked. "Don't forget your hat."

She smiled. "I'll be out in a few."

He accepted that with a nod and headed out the front

door. She quickly returned to her room, went to the bathroom and then slid into her boots and cowboy hat. Taking a quick look in the mirror, she shrugged. *Not half bad, Charly.*

Maybe she could play cowboy after all.

When she made it outside, the morning air was sweet and clear as it filled her lungs. The rising sun peeked over the mountains and washed the ranch in a pale orange glow. She found all the cowboys already mounted, and all eyes came to her—the fake cowboy. She suddenly felt like a filly dropped into the center of a bunch of stallions. And she absolutely hated Aubrey for the dirty thoughts that rushed through her mind.

Though her gaze quickly found Jaxon, and she hurried to his side, handing him her small bag that contained her pajamas and fresh clothes for tomorrow.

His gaze raked over her from head to toe and heated. "Well, well, Kitten, you might just fit in here after all."

She brushed him off with a roll of her eyes. But she didn't hate his comment—she wanted to belong in Timber Falls, her new home. She doubted she'd ever feel truly at home at the ranch—being a city girl—but she longed to feel like she hadn't left her life behind in Phoenix. With near desperation, she wanted to discover this new life was better than she could have ever imagined.

He approached the porch steps and then grabbed up some light gray chaps. "These belonged to one of the cowboys. She was about your size." He offered them to her.

She looked at the worn suede with a frown. "How do you put them on?"

He lifted an eyebrow, a little too full of himself. "I can help you, if you'd like."

She took in all the smiles on the cowboys' faces and sighed. "Yes, please, that'd be great."

She turned away from the group to not let everyone see her face as Jaxon help her into the chaps.

Then he gestured to Thunder. "Up you go."

This time, when he helped her up onto the horse, it seemed far less sexual than last time. Considering the watchful eyes on her, she was glad for it. She took up the reins, as Jaxon stuffed her bag into his saddle bag and then hopped aboard his horse with very little effort.

He turned his horse around and said to the cowboys, "Let's roll out."

The cowboys cheered as they headed off around the barn.

Gunner sidled up to her on a black horse that had white spots on his rump. "Ready for this?"

No. "Absolutely." She smiled.

"Atta girl." He chuckled, riding off.

Eli passed her then, atop his cream-colored horse. "If you need a break, just let me know, and I'll tell them I need to piss." He winked.

Now knowing his tragic past and the loss of his sister, it made his kindness of ensuring she never looked weak even sweeter. "Thanks, Eli. I appreciate that."

He simply nodded and clicked his tongue, sending his horse trotting forward.

She suddenly felt like a massive jerk. Maybe she and her friends had all come here with a chip on their shoulder, but everyone at Timber Falls ranch was kind and growing on her. It made her feel terrible that they weren't doing everything they could to make the locals in town feel as wonderful as they were making the out-of-towners.

"Stick next to me," Jaxon said into the silence, drawing her gaze to him, as he sat atop a pure black horse. "You'll do just fine."

She squeezed her legs and Thunder strode into an easy walk next to Jaxon's horse. "Thunder will do just fine," she said with a laugh. "I will sit here."

Jaxon chuckled and dipped his head. "I'm pretty confident that Thunder could go and bring the horses home without our help at all."

She smiled down at the horse. "He's pretty special, huh?"

"My dad trained him," Jaxon explained, looking way too fine for this early in the morning. He wore a light gray T-shirt, worn jeans and a tan-colored cowboy hat that all fit him with mouth-watering perfection. "Couldn't let him go after, and they were a team for a long time."

"Oh, he was your dad's horse?" she asked, trying to ignore the way his muscles flexed as he lifted the reins, and the large bulging veins running along the sides of his forearms, but she failed miserably.

He inclined his head. "They had quite the bond. When

my dad passed away, I decided to retire Thunder from hard work and let him enjoy his days in the pasture, but we still take him out for some rides to keep him fit and happy."

She stroked Thunder's neck. "Awe, he must miss your dad."

At the silence, she met Jaxon's gaze. His gentle smile was drowned in heartache. "We all do."

For the first time, she felt like she was looking at a side of Jaxon not many got to see. A softer side. She returned the smile. "What was your dad like?"

"He would have liked you," he said with a chuckle, resting the hand holding the reins on the saddle's horn. "My dad appreciated a good woman who could hold her own with a bunch of unruly cowboys."

Her heart fluttered at the compliment. Lately, she'd felt weakened by Marcel's betrayal, feeling like she was anything but strong. "Was your mom a strong woman?" she asked.

"Very much so," Jaxon said, looking as relaxed atop a horse as he did sitting in his chair on the porch last night. "She loved this home and looking after the family and the cowboys on the ranch."

"She used to cook for them?"

"Every day she would serve lunch," he explained. "She loved feeding the guys working on the farm. Everyone loved her."

"Your dad most of all?"

Jaxon laughed. "Yeah, him most of all. They were high school sweethearts."

She let those words sink in, glancing ahead of her, watching as the cowboys continued to head out into the meadow. But her gaze was pulled back to Jaxon. She couldn't quite get how a man raised by two parents who loved each other deeply could not value love and relationships.

"Ask me," he said.

She blinked. "Pardon?"

"You're wondering something," he said. "Ask me."

Her heart squeezed. That felt like a question she wasn't ready for an answer to. Besides, she wasn't there to get to know him. She was there to learn about how to improve their bar to make sure everyone in town was happy and would accept them. "It's nothing. I was just thinking that your parents built something very special here, that's all."

His gaze held hers for a beat, as if he was reading right through her, before glancing ahead of him. "You're right—they did." His expression shifted then, a warm smile filling his face.

She looked out at all the cowboys and their horses again, and a smile spread across her face. "They all look so happy."

Jaxon laughed. "Cowboys live for cowboy shit."

"And what about you?" she asked. "Do you enjoy it?"

Jaxon took a moment to consider her question before answering. "I grew up around here, working on the ranch since I could walk. This is where my roots are, but I had dreams beyond this too. Not saying that I'd ever walk away from the ranch. I just wanted my own accomplishment too. That's why, after saving up enough money, I bought the bar. I enjoyed the late nights, the fun, the regulars—all of it—and I wanted something that belonged to me. Something that I had built and seen succeed."

A twinge of pity touched her. "You did that," she said, feeling the need to ease his loss. "You made the bar successful enough that we bought the business. I wouldn't have bought a failing company."

He gave a warm smile. "Thank you for that, Charly."

She watched him closely, and couldn't help but ask, "Do you ever miss owning the bar?"

He watched his men as they trotted away, laughing and joking with each other. "Not today," he replied with a grin. "Come on, Kitten. You ready to ride?"

"Ready as I'll ever be," she said softly, watching his eyes twinkle as she urged her horse forward.

The smoky fire crackled, and the flames flickered, casting glowing shadows across the meadow. After half a day's trip on horseback over the ranch, they had found the herd of horses near the creek. Beneath the starlit night sky, with its twinkling stars like diamonds in the sky, they had taken off their saddles and Charly had helped them cook up a hearty stew alongside Decker and Cole.

"She did great," Eli commented as he took a seat next to Jaxon, who sat leaning against a tree with a bowl of stew resting in his hands. The hearty concoction—made of beef, potatoes, and onions—was hot and savory, warming his tired body with every bite.

"She's impressive," Jaxon agreed as he watched her scoop more stew into bowls. He hadn't seen her laugh this much. At the bar, she was always so serious, swiping her claws at him. His chest did funny things when he saw her smile and laugh so freely. "She must be exhausted." Riding for two hours is tiring enough for someone inexperienced in horsemanship. She nearly doubled that without complaining once.

The only time he saw any sign of exhaustion was when she dismounted and winced before stretching out her muscles, as if willing strength back into her body.

"If you didn't know better, you'd never guess she was tired," Eli said between bites of stew.

Jaxon nodded. "She's tough."

Eli hummed in agreement before cocking his head. "You like her, hmm?"

"Yeah, I like her," Jaxon answered right away before Gunner came closer. "She's..." He didn't even know how to put what he felt toward her beyond saying, "special."

When Gunner took the other seat next to Jaxon, he said with a chuckle, "Looks like a lot of the cowboys think she's special."

Jaxon snorted. "I've noticed that."

"And they've all seen you glaring," Eli said with a smirk.

"Good. They can get their eyes off her." He'd never admit it aloud, but he enjoyed watching her laugh with the cowboys at the ranch. They were all like family to him.

Some working at the ranch for years. He got why they liked her. He liked her too.

Strong. Sexy. Smart. He loved this game they'd been playing—the bargains they placed at each other's feet to outplay the other, but as he scooped up another spoonful of stew, he was beginning to realize he wanted her again. Not only her body. He wanted to know every bit of her mind.

Eli finally finished his bowl and rose. "I'm calling it a night." He walked over to Gunner, grabbed him by the arm and yanked him up. "And so are you."

Gunner mumbled something incoherent, his mouth full of stew, as Eli dragged him away back to the fire, where the rest of the cowboys remained. Decker sat on one of the logs, strumming on his guitar. He knew eventually Gunner would sink down next to him and the night air would fill with his smooth voice that had captured the world's attention.

"I'm on cleanup duty, boss," Shane suddenly said.

Jaxon handed him his bowl and rose, heading to where his saddle lay on the ground. The rhythmic sound of grass being gently nibbled filled the air, accompanied by the occasional snort or contented sigh from the horses.

He pulled his sweater from the bag and the blanket he'd brought. After returning to Thunder's saddle, he made a pillow from his sweater, leaving the blanket on the saddle for Charly, before returning to his spot leaning against the tree.

His eyes were heavy, the long day wearing on him, but

there wasn't a chance in hell he'd sleep until Charly was next to him and she settled into a deep slumber.

He couldn't take his eyes off her while she leaned against the log, the orange hue from the flickering flames glistening over her skin, as she listened to Decker play.

Two songs later, she yawned, caught him looking at her. He gestured her over with a flick of his chin.

When she reached him, she took in the makeshift bed and asked, "Is this for me?"

He nodded. "It's about as good as it's going to get."

She glanced from her saddle to him and then back again. "Where are you going to sleep?" she eventually asked.

"Against my saddle," he said, which happened to be set right next to hers.

He waited for her uproar but was surprised when she pulled out a sweater from her bag and put it on. Then she just lay down, adjusting his sweater into a tighter pillow against the angled saddle and pulled the blanket over her. "Thanks. I appreciate the bed, even if it's not much of one."

He wondered if her lack of refusal to sleep next to him came from being nervous about being outside and feeling safer next to him. Or she wanted him close too. He liked either of those choices. He smiled. "You're welcome."

She curled up on her side and stared at him.

He watched her back and wasn't surprised when he heard Gunner's voice as he began singing, obviously taking over the guitar. Though the song wasn't familiar. Maybe something new, Jaxon wondered.

Charly lifted her head, watching Gunner a moment. "He's got quite the voice, doesn't he?"

"He's been talented like that since we were kids," Jaxon explained. "There was never any doubt he'd go into music."

She lowered her head back to her makeshift pillow, her hand sliding under her cheek.

He'd never cared much what people thought of him, but it grated on his last nerve that she thought he had a long list of red flags. "Can I ask where you heard that I was a guy you needed to stay away from?"

She stayed silent for so long he thought she wasn't going to answer. Then she surprised him as she said, "I was warned about you at the bar. It's not like they said awful things about you, just said that you're not careful with a woman's heart."

He huffed, glancing up to the starry sky. He understood why some women might view him that way, but that was because they didn't know him. Not truly. Yeah, he was no saint, but he'd never played with a woman's heart. "What I think is a player is a man who doesn't care who he hurts. That's not me. It wasn't ever me."

"But you did play around?"

He met her gaze again and shrugged, refusing to lie to her no matter if it made him look bad. "When my dad died and I lost my bar, I was in a dark place. The dream I had worked for, and thought would be *my* legacy had been taken away. Drinking and women filled that void for a while. I'm not proud of it. But I never made anyone any promises. I never dated. I had casual sex. That was all that was on the table."

She didn't take her eyes off him. "So then why are women so salty about you?"

He hesitated, wondering if he should stick to truth. He figured it might scare her away, but he couldn't seem to not want to stop pushing forward with her. "Jealously is my guess."

"Jealous of who?"

He held her gaze, laying it all on the line. Screw the consequences. "The pretty brunette that I couldn't take my eyes off of the entire time I was in the bar."

Her brows drew together until realization hit her that he was talking about her. "Oh."

He loved that little surprise on her face. "In all seriousness, I can't speak for the women in my past," he said, liking how she was holding his stare, not looking away from him. "Was I straight up with my intentions? Yes. Was I always kind? Probably not. But I never made promises and I never crossed emotional lines."

Her eyes searched his for a long moment. "Have you ever had a serious relationship?" she eventually asked.

"During high school I had a girlfriend for most of it," he explained, resting his arm behind his head. "But that was young love. It ended when she went to college, and she never moved back to town."

"There was no one after that?" she asked.

"I dated Lauren for a year before I opened the bar, but that didn't end well."

"Why is that?"

"Because I was too busy getting the bar going to focus on a relationship," he explained. "She didn't appreciate being put second all the time, and I can't blame her for that."

A soft wind swept through the branches of the trees, stirring up a quiet rustle of leaves. "Do you miss her?" she asked. "What you had with her, I mean?"

He turned his head, stared at her firmly. "There is only one woman that I want to be looking at right now."

Her expression revealed nothing, before she glanced toward Gunner, who sang into the night.

Realizing she wasn't going to comment on that, he switched the subject, curious about her. "What about you? Do you have heartbroken exes in your past?"

She laughed softly. "That's highly unlikely. I've had two boyfriends in my life. One broke up with me for reasons I still don't really know. And well, you know about Marcel."

Yeah, he did. He'd like a few minutes alone with him too. Though he was curious about where she stood with him. "Have you forgiven Marcel for what he did to you?"

She snorted, meeting his gaze again. "That's a loaded question."

"It's a curious question," he countered.

"I don't think I need to forgive him," she said after a moment of thought. "I think forgiveness should be for people who love you. Truly love you. What Marcel did is unforgivable, meaning he doesn't deserve to be in my life. Leaving him was more about moving on than forgiving him."

He found that highly unlikely. "You've moved on?"

Her lips parted to reply but then they shut. She glanced up at the stars above her, and he could see her eyes growing watery. "How do you move on from something like that? I'm starting over...and really, that's all I can think of to do."

"Do you still talk to him?"

"I talked to him once just recently to tell him to let me move on, but now I've blocked him," she said. "There's nothing he could say that could help with my healing and I refuse to be a sounding board to help him feel better from what he ruined."

Asking the same question she had him, he asked, "Do you miss him?"

She looked to the sky again and sighed. "I miss the life I thought we had. I miss who I was when I was with him. I was unflappable, trusted without thought and had a clear vision of my future. This new me..." Her gaze fell to his, her mouth shutting like she was about to spill secrets to him she hadn't mean to.

"This new you?" he pressed.

Her voice shook a little. "I don't even know myself anymore."

He turned onto his side, holding her stare. He'd never believed in the magic in the mountains or the legend, but as he stared into the fiery depths of Charly's eyes, feeling things he'd never felt with any woman, he'd wondered if he'd been wrong. "You're the woman who got on a plane and started a new life, no matter how hard it must have been. The same person who's generous enough to celebrate women all so they can feel pride in themselves and yet rides a horse all day long with a bunch of foul-mouthed cowboys without complaining once—all to better understand people and make them happy. I'm just starting to get to know you, and I can't take my eyes off you." He wasn't thinking, only acting on need, when he leaned forward and kissed her forehead, before looking her in the eyes again. "If you ever doubt how incredible you are, talk to me, I'll set you right. I've never met anyone like you and I'm damn glad to know you."

He waited for her to respond. When she didn't, obviously stunned a little speechless, he smiled, probably cockily in the way she hated, and he settled in next to her, laying his head back against the saddle. He slid his hat over his eyes. "Good night, Charly."

A long moment passed. Then her soft voice drifted over him. "Good night, Jaxon."

Eleven

Charly had secretly wished that everyone overslept and woke up at a more civil hour the following morning, but that wasn't in the cards. Despite her conviction that no one had set an alarm, Charly was proven wrong as everyone rose ahead of sunrise. While she shoved the blanket back into the bag, it suddenly hit her—she wasn't a cowboy and would never be. She wasn't built to wake up at this hour.

The journey back home took just as long as the ride out, although this time around Jaxon kept her busy by teaching her how to herd the horses that had strayed from the group. A task easier than expected since Thunder seemed to understand his job better than she did.

By late afternoon they had all returned to the ranch. She sat atop Thunder, watching as the cowboys herded the horses into a large pen. The more she watched them do their thing, the more Charly realized how hard cowboys worked. She had put in long days and nights at the bar and knew the difficulties of such labor. However, this kind of physical work seemed utterly exhausting. Fortunately, they had perfect weather, but even if it had been pouring rain, she knew these cowboys would have soldiered on without complaint.

She suddenly felt she was the enemy as she thought about the bar they no longer enjoyed. She and the girls had unintentionally taken away a place they had loved. She'd stripped the place of what made Timber Falls, Timber Falls. All the rustic elements she had thought were meaningless meant everything to them. And country music wasn't only music to them, it was a way of life. She'd stolen away a place they could let off steam or just have fun with drinks and friends after their long day. Unknowingly, they had deprived them of something that made them happy.

Feeling about two feet tall now, she filled the two coffee mugs from the machine installed by Jaxon on his porch and then she walked up to him. He was standing near the sand ring with Eli, who was typing on a laptop beside him, and Gunner was clutching a clipboard of papers.

She handed Jaxon the steaming mug of black coffee. "Thought you might like this," she said.

He looked at it and beamed gratefully. "Thanks, I do." He took a sip and closed his eyes in satisfaction.

Her mind slipped away, no matter how hard she tried to fight it. She remembered the last time he had looked so contented, hearing his throaty groan in her ears as he spilled onto her. She cleared her throat quickly, her heart thudding against her ribs. "So, what exactly are you doing here?" she asked, settling in next to him.

"We're picking which horses will stay here at the ranch for training or breeding and which ones will go up for auction tomorrow," he explained.

From the two groups, all the horses looked pretty similar to her, but had different colors and markings. "How do you decide which ones to keep and which ones to sell?" she asked.

"We choose horses based on confirmation," Jaxon explained, as if she should understand what he meant. She didn't as he continued, "They need to have no structural flaws in their necks, shoulders, backs, or hips. Plus, their spines should be shorter than their underlines."

She blinked. "I never would have guessed so much thought went into this."

Jaxon hesitated, before hitting her with an emotion-packed smile. "My dad believed in quality horses that came from good breeding. It's something I intend to carry on until the day I die."

She returned the smile and stepped back, sipping her coffee, and observing them all working hard. The complexity of Jaxon's business surprised her. Watching him work made her realize just how impressive the ranch was and, if his dad were around, she felt certain he'd feel nothing but pride for his son.

His strong character began to outshine all the captivating physical traits she couldn't stop noticing.

As a few more hours whizzed by, Charly remained fascinated as all the horses were catalogued and turned into two smaller groups of horses. One group stayed in the large pen, who were happily eating hay that the cowboys had fed them. The other group was put in a large pasture where they'd stay until training or breeding began.

When the final horse was sorted, a catering company arrived, setting out salads and pulled pork sandwiches. The air wafted with the scent of charcoal, smoke, meat and spices, and Charly's belly rumbled.

Jaxon left his place at the sand ring, and said to her, "Let's go grab some grub, Kitten."

The contempt she felt for the nickname yesterday had dwindled, perhaps due to the warm timbre of his voice when he said it.

Soon she found herself seated in the grass among sweaty, dirt-caked cowboys who were all smiling from ear-to-ear. The conversation was easy and lighthearted as jokes flew around.

Until Decker asked Charly, "How's the bar going?"

Charly felt every set of eyes on her as she swallowed the food in her mouth. It surprised her this hadn't come up sooner. "It's going all right. Thanks for asking, Decker," she replied.

"Good to hear." He gave a slight nod and his lips

twitched. "What are the chances of getting the pool tables back in?"

"Um…" Charly looked around at the cowboys before focusing on Decker. "Is that what you miss most about the bar?"

One of the other cowboys coughed, muttering something beneath his breath, but Decker ignored him and only nodded. "It's a start."

A few chuckles came from among the group.

Charly found herself in an unexpected situation, as these men all seemed eager to give her honest feedback. She set her sandwich down on her plate and told them, "All right then, let me have it—tell me everything you miss about the bar."

Everyone turned toward Jaxon.

He frowned, midway from taking a bite of his sandwich. "Why are you looking at me? I didn't ask the question."

Rolling her eyes, convinced they were worried he'd deck them if they upset her, Charly said, "I mean it, I want to know—tell me everything."

"Okay, then," Decker said with a shrug. "If you say so…"

Twenty minutes later, she wished she'd never said anything as they hit her with all their various complaints. From missing dartboards to a lack of available single women who didn't want to claw out their eyeballs. To the choice of music, beer, and bar food.

To the heart of it, Charly knew they wanted Jaxon's bar back again.

She sighed, trying to sort through what they wanted and trying to mesh that with the vision she, Willow and Aubrey had for the bar.

As if Jaxon saw her struggle, he stood up abruptly and slid his hat back onto his head. "That's enough bitching for one day," he announced before turning to face Charly again, offering his hand. "Let's get back to work."

She took his hand, rose and had the feeling he didn't want to let go. Oddly, she felt her fingers twitch to hold on, before she pulled away, tossing her empty plate in the garbage. "You guys aren't done for the day?" she asked.

Amused laughter spread around her again, telling her everything she needed to know about how serious Jaxon was being right now.

Naturally, he explained himself further, "We still have to brand all of the horses with our freeze brand."

Charly cocked her head. "Which is what exactly?"

Jaxon gestured toward the dozen coolers that had metal rods inside which lined the paddock fence and said, "Come here and I'll show you."

Jaxon grabbed one of the rods and showed it off—a logo shaped like a "T" intertwined with an "F and R." Pointing at it, he said, "We use this to brand the horses to mark them as Timber Falls Ranch Quarter Horses."

Her hand instinctively flew to her chest. "Does it hurt them?" she asked.

He shook his head in response. "No, not nearly as much as being fire branded would. It's quick and easy." He pointed to the long metal fencing, resembling a tunnel. "We place the horse in the chute there, and after a few seconds, the procedure destroys the natural pigmentation of the hair."

"So that's what makes the hair turn white?" She'd seen the mark on Thunder. She stepped closer to get a better look, trailing beside him toward the chute.

He nodded and smiled. "It serves as a badge of pride for all horses from Timber Falls Ranch."

Staying behind the fence, she watched as the cowboys rounded up the auction horses and moved them to a smaller pen before pushing them through the chute one by one. Each horse was branded before they sent them on their way. Not even one showed any pain, mostly looked startled at first, but they were out of the chute before they even registered it.

"A brand of honor, huh?" she said.

He nodded. "That logo means something around here." Then, he gestured toward the chute. "Do you want to give it a try?"

She'd come this far and figured she couldn't stop now. "Hell yeah!" She followed Jaxon around to where a horse the color of dark chocolate stood in the chute. She watched as Decker shaved a spot on the side of the horse's rump and then Casey washed it, before pouring a liquid on it. "What's he putting on there?" Charly asked.

"It's ninety-nine percent alcohol." Jaxon reached into the cooler and grabbed one of the rods, offering her the end with the handle. "When I say, you press that where I show you for thirty seconds."

"Okay." She stepped closer to where she'd seen the other cowboys standing when they did this part.

Casey finished the wipe down, backed away and Jaxon nodded her on. "All right, you're on."

She closed the distance, raised the brand, aiming where Jaxon was pointing.

"Hold for thirty seconds," he said.

"Got it." She leaned in, just inches away, but instantly pulled back. "No, I can't, I'm going to hurt it."

"He'll be a little sore for fifteen minutes, but the pain will fade," Jaxon said in a reassuring tone. "He'll be out of the chute before he even knows what happens. He won't even flinch. Trust me, horses are tough."

She gave him a *look*. "I bet some animal activists would disagree with you."

He chuckled. "I have no doubt about that." He gestured her on with a firm nod. "Now or never."

She leaned forward again, the cold rod nearly on the horse's body, and froze again. "Nope, I can't do it," she gasped.

Jaxon stepped in behind her, running his hands down her arms. "You're causing the horse more stress by taking so long rather than just stamping its ass."

The thought horrified her as much as branding him. She screamed and pressed the rod against the horse. Jaxon was right, the horse didn't even flinch, as Jaxon stroked the horse's back, and like Jaxon said, he was out of the chute and on his way without much fuss.

"Take the rod," she said, her arms shaking. "I never want to do that again."

Jaxon laughed, coming up behind her, taking the rod from her hands. He pressed his strength against her and murmured in her ear, "Now you're a real cowboy."

She nearly told him that she was most certainly not, but her brain stuttered. She wasn't thinking about the branding anymore. She was only thinking that if she turned her head just a little she'd capture his lips.

And *that* was a problem.

Jaxon moved through his silent home long after all the cowboys were gone. He had heard Charly shower before he showered himself, but he wasn't ready to say goodbye to her yet. Tomorrow she was going home after the auction.

But he still had tonight.

His only goal was to ensure she left his house with a better opinion of him than when she arrived. Because the more time he spent with her, the more he knew he wanted more.

He soon reached the guest bedroom, and he rapped on the door, hearing her moving around inside.

When she opened the door, he had to fight against giving her a full once-over—especially when he saw how little she was wearing, only a long T-shirt. His cock stirred instantly. *Damn it, this woman...*

He wrenched his eyes back up to her face and asked, "Would you like to come with me somewhere?"

"Right now?" she replied with wide eyes.

"Yeah." He looked her over again. "You should probably get dressed first."

Her cheeks turned crimson as if she just realized she wasn't wearing very much and she had no bra, revealing taut nipples. "Give me a few minutes," she said quickly.

Before she shut the door, he said, "I'll meet you outside. Put on something comfy and a sweater."

"Okay." She quickly closed the door, and he swore he heard her talking to herself.

Smiling to himself, he headed away before his urges got the best of him and he pulled her onto the bed.

Once outside, greeted by a gorgeous clear night, he untied Thunder and his mount from the porch and made sure their saddles were secure. Charly had come out soon after, looking just as sexy in jeans and an oversized hoodie, her hair pulled back into a ponytail.

Maybe this wasn't a good idea. How in the hell was he going to keep his hands off her?

The last thing he wanted to do was get those claws all up in his face again. Finally, he felt like they'd gotten somewhere. Her smile came easier. Her sweet laughter filled his ears. She fit right into his life, and he liked how he felt with her around.

"Are we going for a ride?" she asked, coming down the stairs.

He nodded. "If that's all right with you."

She smiled, finally reaching him. "That's all right with me."

"Great." He gave her a lift onto Thunder's back and then mounted his own horse.

After he gathered up his reins, he noted how much more comfortable she looked atop Thunder now. "All set?"

She nodded silently and he clicked his tongue sending his mount forward at a walk. Charly and Thunder kept pace beside them.

"You do know it's dark out here," she said.

Chuckling, he replied, "I could find my way around this land blindfolded and get home without a problem." He looked up at the starry sky above before he grinned at her. "No speaking for the rest of the ride—just enjoy it."

She pretended to zip her lips shut and smiled.

He let the quiet settle in and savored the surrounding sights. It had been ages since he'd gone on a nighttime ride like this. The last time was with Gunner and Eli before Gunner went on touring the world. Now, older, it felt vastly different...*quieter.*

The horses' hooves crushed against the tall grass beneath them as crickets sang their tune. He stayed silent, wanting her to experience Montana's vast beauty when the world went quiet, until they reached the top of the mountain range and Thunder slowed to a halt right next to him.

"Look up," he said.

"Wow," she breathed out in awe. "Oh, wow. I have never seen so many stars in my life."

He followed her gaze, taking in the spectacular view for himself. Nothing could compare to seeing such magnificence up in the sky, and he'd never seen the stars so bright anywhere else he'd gone. Not when he'd visited Gunner on the road, or went out to spend a weekend with Eli in the big city.

Nowhere compared to Timber Falls.

"I can see why some believe there is a legend attached to this place," she eventually stated, still staring upward. "It's incredibly magical."

"That it is," he concurred.

After hopping down from his horse, he extracted a blanket from his saddlebag and unfolded it out along the ground before helping her dismount from Thunder too. He secured both horses to a tree and waved for her to come over and lie down beside him on the blanket. She did so, looking up into the stars above with a long sigh.

He got that too. Somehow the heaviness of life was gone with a simple exhale.

"Thank you for bringing me here," she murmured after a long while, turning her head toward him while crossing her arms behind her head as a cushion. "And thank you for introducing me to the ranch and showing me everything. I feel like I have a better understanding of people here in town."

"You're welcome," he replied with a smile. "I'm glad you came."

Part of him wanted to fill the silence with all the questions he had running through his mind concerning her, but another part of him knew she probably needed a few moments to herself—out there, peace was found.

"I had my doubts about moving here to Timber Falls," she said in the silent night air. "Regardless if I had a million reasons to leave the city."

He peered over and saw her gentle expression under the moonbeams. "Why?"

"Honestly, I just wasn't sure that we were doing the right thing," she said. "We'd worked so hard for the lives we created. Timber Falls is so opposite of what we knew. Life here is so different."

"Maybe that's what makes it so great," he offered.

"Maybe," she agreed with a nod, "but I was honestly terrified that I wasn't only ruining my life but ruining Aubrey and Willow's lives moving here. I was the one who created the pact. I was the one who called it in and said we should move here. There was just so much on the line. We sold everything. We put all our savings into starting this new life here." She paused to draw in a long breathe. "For weeks, I've had this lump in my throat, feeling like at any second the ball would drop, and we'd realize we made a massive mistake."

He was transfixed by her honesty and openness. "And now?"

"Now…" Her gaze fixed on him, and something sweet and pure passed between them. "I think this is where I was always meant to be."

He couldn't take his eyes off her. The peaceful happiness on her face was the most beautiful thing he'd ever seen in his life. "Why do you think that?"

She paused, looking to the stars again as if they held all the answers. "I don't know, just…it feels…"

"Right," he offered.

She nodded, turning her head to meet his gaze again. "Yeah, it feels right."

He agreed, feeling the same way when she was by his side. He'd never felt this level of comfort with any woman. Hell, he wasn't sure he'd felt it with anyone before.

She watched his face carefully and then asked, "Is it always like this out here?"

"Like what?"

"Healing…"

He gave her a knowing look and smile. "The mountains are magical, remember. Healing comes naturally here."

Holding his stare, she dragged a deep breath of air before blowing it out, looking back up to the sky. "Life takes strange turns, doesn't it? I thought my life would be one way, but suddenly it changed shape into something else entirely."

He chuckled softly. "That's something I'm familiar with."

She glanced over at him, her eyes shining in the moonlight. "Do you think you'll miss what your old dream was?"

He paused for a moment before answering. "For a while I did, but then I realized an old dream has to die so a new one can live in its place." Like all the stars were aligning, it felt like giving up on his dream brought her to him, and he'd never regret that.

A gentle smile crossed her lips and he felt warmth spread through his chest. He rolled onto his side so he could look down at her, needing to erase the distance between them. As he ran his fingers through her hair, she didn't pull away as he'd expected. Instead, she stayed rooted to the spot as she gazed into his eyes with an intensity that overwhelmed him. He murmured quietly, "I like you."

She laughed softly. "Do you?"

He nodded and dragged his finger along her jawline, reveling in the feel of her silky skin beneath his fingertips. "Yes, I do. I like how brave you are. You didn't let heartbreak define you. You created a new life for yourself. I like how you fight to help others feel special and powerful. I like how you listened to my cowboys to understand the locals. I like how I feel when I'm around you."

"How do you feel?" she asked.

He brushed his knuckles across her cheek. "Like I can't look anywhere else but at you. I feel…happy."

A long pause followed, but she managed to surprise him by saying gently, "I like you too, Jaxon. I like your strong character. I like how you treat your friends and cowboys. I like that you walked away from your dream for your family. I like how you see the world like it's a gift, not something that you can constantly take from. I like how I feel when I'm around you too."

He smiled as she used his words back on him. "How do you feel?"

"Happy," she said. "Even when I should feel like I've lost everything."

He'd been used to taking pleasure from women without feeling anything—but this time something was different, and he wanted to take a step back and do things slowly. Because he wanted to see and feel all of this woman.

His gaze traced down to her lips. This was what he wanted, more than anything else. "Can I kiss you?" he asked while caressing her jawline with his knuckles.

"What do I get if I let you?" she asked, playfully.

He chuckled. Another bargain was fine by him. "A kiss that sets you on fire isn't enough?"

She laughed softly, her pretty eyes twinkling at him, shaking her head.

"Hmm," he said, brushing his thumb against her bottom lip. "How about a single wish to be used at your discretion, whenever you see fit."

The amusement faded from her expression, replaced by a heat so overpowering his breath caught in his chest. "Deal," she rasped.

He moved closer and slowly pressed his mouth against hers—soft and sweet like he imagined.

He savored how her lips felt against his and the desire that flooded through him as they kissed deeper and deeper.

Asking for permission with a lick of his tongue, she complied by opening her mouth and letting him explore further. Cupping her face with both hands, he deepened the kiss and elicited a moan from her.

When the kiss intensified, she leaned in and allowed it to grow more passionate. He groaned in pleasure as his hand moved to her waist and drew her body closer, bringing all that heat against him.

He grunted against the taste of her, and she pulled away. "Jaxon, I don't—"

"It's okay." He silenced her with a finger over her lips and pleaded, "Just let me kiss you, Charly. That's all I want."

"Just kissing?" she whispered.

He brushed his mouth across hers. "Just...*this*." Then he sealed his mouth across hers and lost himself in her sweetness.

Twelve

Midmorning the next day, the fluffy clouds scattered the sky, casting long shadows over the bustling crowd around the ranch. Charly stood near the auction ring, taking it all in. The sound of laughter and chatter filled the air, mingling with the aroma of smoky barbecue wafting from the nearby food tent. The atmosphere was electric, pulsating with excitement and she saw what the fuss was all about.

The auction wasn't only about selling horses, it was about tradition. Every person who talked to Jaxon seemed like they'd known him for his entire life. There was a certain type of magic there, where people were celebrating Montana ranch living and the beauty of horses.

She settled in next to Gunner at the fence line, who stood beside Eli, and asked, "This is kind of his thing, huh?"

"Yeah," said Gunner, watching Jaxon as he shook a cowboy's hand. "Always been. He's good with a crowd."

"It's what made the bar successful," Eli added. "People like him."

She became trapped in Jaxon's smile as he spoke with the cowboy in front of him. She got it. She liked him too, even though everything in her head was telling her she had no business liking or kissing anyone so soon after her last relationship ended.

A dark horse was led into the round pen set up in front of the stage, where the auctioneer stood behind a podium.

His voice boomed through the speakers. "Look at this filly. She's got all the chrome. Let's start the bidding at six thousand."

Bidders leaned in, their eyes fixed on the horse, studying every line of the horse's body and demeanor; clad in cowboy boots and hats, they shared animated conversations and hearty laughs. Charly couldn't help but be drawn to their contagious enthusiasm.

As the bidding escalated, she watched as one bidder had determination etched on his face. The atmosphere crackled with anticipation as the bidding war unfolded. Until the gavel struck, sealing the deal for eight thousand dollars as the final bid.

The victorious bidder's face lit up with an ecstatic smile, their eyes sparkling with a mix of pride and excitement. They exchanged high fives and hugs with their friends, who cheered them on.

"Good grief," Charly said. "I had no idea horses were so expensive."

Eli chuckled. "In the horse world, Charly, eight thousand is pocket change."

But as she glanced from face to face it became clear that this went beyond the business of the auction, this gathering was a celebration of the profound connection between humans and horses, and what Timber Falls Ranch stood for in this world.

The thought had stayed with her for the rest of the day, even when she finally arrived at the bar to work, as did thoughts of all that Jaxon stood for. Blind faith had gotten her heart broken before, but she couldn't help but see that beneath Jaxon's shield was the pain he secretly kept hidden. Buried beneath layers of responsibility not to tarnish his father's legacy and to see the ranch continue to succeed. Most of all, she saw his red flags evaporating. It became glaringly obvious that Jaxon was an honorable man. A good man. One worthy of being given a chance.

"What are you thinking about?" Aubrey inquired, bringing Charly back from her trancelike gaze out the bar window.

"Oh, I was just thinking about how everything seems so different since I had my little stint as a cowboy," she explained, glancing at Aubrey, who wore a cute flower-patterned sundress with ballet flats, with her hair in a fishtail braid.

Aubrey gave a tender smile. "You definitely look different after your stay at the ranch…happier too, certainly."

Charly nodded in agreement. She understood that during these last days her defenses had dropped, and she'd finally allowed herself to embrace what had been happening between her and Jaxon without resisting it anymore.

Although the fear of vulnerability still lingered beneath her skin, she decided to push it aside and let the feelings take over. She was done trying to carefully think out every situation and trying to determine the correct decisions. She didn't want to dive headfirst into anything with him, but she also wasn't pushing away what was beginning to build between them either.

"Not only that," she eventually responded to Aubrey, "but I think we got it right here too."

It wasn't even happy hour, and the bar was completely packed. After she talked with the cowboys about the bar, she'd sent the girls a text about their wishes. While Charly was at the ranch, Willow and Aubrey made some changes. They brought a couple pool tables in and a dart board. They also rearranged the schedule. From Monday to Wednesday, they would hold party nights to help with heartaches and celebrate successes, but the rest of the week now belonged to the town. They brought in live music and tonight had been their busiest night yet, filled with line dancers and partiers looking for their match, or just to dance the night away.

The country music competed with the loud voices and laughter throughout the space. And the place was full of locals.

Aubrey scanned the area and give a firm nod. "Well, one thing is for sure," she said, meeting Charly's gaze again. "Everyone seems happy."

"They do," Charly agreed.

Willow came from the back carrying a box of beer and knelt by the fridge, restocking it with a half dozen different kinds of craft beers. "I can't believe how busy it already is," she remarked.

"We were just talking about that," Aubrey said, handing Willow the bottles from the box. "Seems like tonight might be when we get it right for this town."

"We owe that to Jaxon," Charly noted, knowing her time at the ranch gave her insight into the truth about the locals: they loved their ladies, live music, and good beer. Add in a pool table and dart board, and they would never complain.

As if on cue, Jaxon entered the bar accompanied by Eli and Gunner. He gave them each a nod and sat down on a stool. "Hi, ladies," he said.

"Foxy Divas?" Willow asked, offering their favorite craft beer, seemingly focusing only on Eli, as he sat next to Jaxon, while Gunner took the other stool.

He nodded with a smile in her direction.

Charly felt that he was kind and harmless; maybe even good for Willow, even though she wasn't looking for romance right now.

"Beers up!" Aubrey announced as she slid each a bottle across the bar.

"Thanks." Gunner grinned, glancing around before meeting their gazes again. "Place looks great."

Aubrey smiled. "Happy cowboys, happy life, am I right?"

Gunner winked. "Sounds about right to me."

Aubrey turned away, seemingly unaffected by Gunner's charm that Charly had seen make women nearly melt into puddles at his feet.

Charly's heart skipped a beat when Jaxon leaned over the

bar and planted a kiss on her lips, like he'd done it a million times before now. Even she had to admit having him kiss her in public didn't feel awkward. Which was odd— shouldn't that feel uncomfortable?

He trailed his mouth near her ear and murmured, "You look beautiful, Charly."

She forced herself not to blush in front of everyone. She'd also never admit that she wore the tight skinny jeans and short blouse all to tease him tonight. "Thank you," she replied. "Now, join your friends on the other side of the bar or else I'll throw you out myself."

He chuckled before returning to his stool and taking a long swig of his beer.

Aubrey and Willow both had huge grins on their faces. The same ones they made whenever Jaxon showed up.

Charly rolled her eyes at them and mouthed: *stop it!*

Jaxon set his beer back down. "What's the plan for tomorrow?" he asked.

"The plan is to have a quiet night after we close," Charly said.

"What about heading coming to the ranch for drinks and a fire?" Jaxon asked, addressing Willow and Aubrey too. "Eli and Gunner are coming too, plus a few others."

Willow glanced at Eli, who nodded.

"I'm in!" Aubrey exclaimed, nearly bouncing on her feet. "I'm dying for some fun."

Charly couldn't help laughing in agreement. She missed a night out too. All they'd been doing is working.

"Great!" Jaxon continued, a pleased grin on his face.

"Come by after you close. I can arrange a taxi to take you home afterward, okay? Or if you'd like, you're welcome to stay the night at my place."

Charly refused to let the heat rise to her cheeks at that tempting thought. She still felt that kiss last night right down to her toes, burning across her lips, like a sensual promise hanging in the balance.

"I'll bring snacks to eat on the way," Willow offered with a beaming smile.

Eli turned away and coughed awkwardly. Oh, yeah, Eli thought Willow was a little snack herself.

Charly smiled to herself, hardly able to believe it. They were settled, and dare she say happy. She'd gone from loathing men to wanting Jaxon. She expected the worry to bubble up over starting over, but it never came. Timber Falls had welcomed them with new friendships and a fresh start, and Charly felt grateful this crazy plan had all come together and somehow worked out in the end.

Even now, Jaxon's stare held hers like she was the only one that mattered in this room, and it felt so damn good to feel special again. Her heart fluttered as she stepped around the bar and moved to his stool, interrupting him midsentence. She grabbed his chin and kissed him—lingering until he opened his mouth to her, slipping her tongue against his.

She didn't care who was watching and even wanted everyone to see it. To know they were more than just friends, even if they hadn't put a label on it yet. She kissed him passionately, moving her tongue against his in a sensual rhythm that made her toes curl in pleasure.

When she finally pulled away from him, she saw the raw desire in his eyes, and felt it deep in her core.

"What was that for?" he murmured, brushing his thumb against her bottom lip.

"That cowboy charm is in full force tonight," she replied with a smirk, "I need to get a new bottle of whiskey. I'll be back." She spun around but was stopped by his strong arms wrapping around her waist.

"We'll finish this later," he whispered huskily into her ear, causing shivers to run down her spine.

She reluctantly peeled herself off him and went to grab the new bottle of whiskey, hot everywhere that craved his touch most.

After she grabbed the bottle from the back room, she pushed the door open, smiling to herself.

One look at the bar, and her smile immediately dropped.

Jaxon sat on his stool with a beautiful brunette draped over him, making Charly feel underdressed and inadequate, a feeling that was hauntingly familiar. Her gaze followed the woman's finger as it traced along Jaxon's bicep while he did nothing to stop her advances.

All the warnings of Jaxon's red flags came rushing back, mixed with awareness that once again she hadn't been enough for a man, taunting her for being so foolish.

Charly sucked in a breath and did the only thing she could think to do.

She ran.

Thirteen

The warmth wrapping around Jaxon from behind was the exact type of warmth he used to crave—purely physical. But now his emotions were involved, making the touch mean so much more. He turned his head, expecting to find Charly, and instantly jerked away when he realized it wasn't her nuzzling into him. In fact, she was a woman he'd taken to his bed a couple times in the past—Samantha.

Worse, he connected with Charly's eyes as she glared his way. He caught her hurt expression as she fled to the back room.

With his anger growing, he rose, putting distance between him and Samantha, and growled at her, "What are you doing?"

"Making this easy for you," she said with a sultry smirk. "Let's get out of here."

Eli coughed awkwardly, while Gunner snickered.

"Do not touch me again," Jaxon said as he watched her take a step back in shock.

He heard Eli explain to Samantha that he was taken, but he wasn't even sure if that was true. All he knew was he was walking a thin line already to impress Charly, and he'd just burned that line up.

Shoving aside his hesitation to step into the back room considering he didn't own the place anymore, he rushed off to find Charly. The swinging door flapped behind him as he peered into the kitchen and then the office, but finding nothing, until he spotted her through the window of the back door, looking toward the road.

He hurried out the door, entering the empty alleyway, which was illuminated by the soft glow of distant streetlights. A sense of calm crept over him as he stepped into the narrow passage between the old brick buildings. The warm night air enveloped him, and it felt like a world away from the bar. He stopped a few feet away from her, facing her palpable anger.

"Charly," was all he could manage when he reached her.

She breathed heavily and spat out, "I'm so damn sick of men thinking they can just trample over me."

He softened his tone as he implored, "Charly, look at me."

But she wouldn't have it, striding away from him, heading toward the road. The thought of her getting away sent a shot of fear through him which spurred him on to reach out and grab her wrist. "It's not what you think," he pleaded.

She whirled around and glared at him, her voice scathing. "Let me guess, she grabbed you, and you felt nothing for her?"

"Not quite." He stepped closer to her, taking a firm hold of her waist as he did so, ensuring she wouldn't leave him. "It's unfortunate that you came out the same time she was coming close to me, but I assumed it was you. When I realized it wasn't, I dealt with it."

Charly's nostrils flared in anger. "And yet she was touching you."

He shrugged, not wanting to let go of her waist. He understood her anger. Someone had betrayed her. Those feelings lingered. "If you had stayed, you would have seen that it didn't last long."

Her eyes narrowed. "It doesn't matter…you're…you are…" She inhaled sharply then growled, "You're the devil. From day one, you've always been the devil in blue jeans."

He held her gaze for a moment before erupting into laughter at her expression of fury.

"I'm going to hurt you," she declared.

Before she could swear again, he pulled her into his arms and cupped her face gently. "Kitten, I like you and those claws of yours so damn much." She went to step back. He tightened his hold. "Would you just stop?" he asked, unable to keep the smile off his face. "You're the only woman I came here to see tonight. I want no one else's hands on me—only yours."

Her nostrils flared. "How can I trust that? She was all over you."

"Because I am not in the alleyway with her," he said. "I'm here with you, and you're the only one I want. That's it. Full stop."

Then before she could respond, he kissed her, half convinced she would knock him a good one. She remained tense but didn't move away. He softened the kiss, tangling his fingers into her hair to angle her head, deepening the kiss.

He kissed her until she believed him. Until sighs of pleasure were on her lips instead of curses. Until she was all but crawling up his body for more. He kissed until she knew beyond any doubt she was the only one he wanted.

"Convinced?" he asked, kissing the soft skin at her throat.

"No, I don't think so," she rasped. Gone was the anger in her voice, replaced by something much more needy as she moaned when his tongue found an especially sensitive spot. She ran her hands up his biceps. "You better keep trying to convince me."

"Hmm…is that so?" he mused, nipping at the skin at the base of her neck.

He kissed his way up her neck, until his mouth was level with hers. He gave in to temptation and took possession of her lips, knowing she wanted him as much as he wanted her. He could feel it against his mouth, against his body, and with every eager moan she gave. She knocked his cowboy hat off before sliding her hands into his hair, holding him tight. He moaned, pressing the heavy weight of his erection against her stomach, running his hands down over her breasts before settling firmly on her waist and moving her back and away from prying eyes. The alleyway wasn't very well lit, and he'd placed her in one corner hidden by a wall and crates blocking the view. Keeping his hands firmly on her waist he gently nudged her until her back hit the wall in that shadowed spot.

He looked down into her face. "I better rectify that then," he murmured.

Her eyes reflected lust and longing, and he licked his lips before kissing her with force.

The overwhelming compulsion to touch her, explore her, consume her enveloped him and spun him into a whirlwind of need. He pulled her toward him and sucked at the sensitive spot on her neck, his breath echoing her heady moans. His hands roamed hungrily over her body until they found their target. He grasped a firm handful of her bottom as she pressed against his rigid length.

A low groan rolled from deep within his chest as he leaned back and commanded huskily, "Take those down for me, Kitten, will you?" She complied eagerly, tugging down her skinny jeans that had him nearly drooling. In one swift motion he dropped his jeans and rolled on a condom.

In that moment there was nothing but raw desire between them. Every instinct in his body begged him to take his time savoring every inch of her smooth skin, yet they were far too exposed here. If they were discovered, the whole town would know about it tomorrow. He wouldn't do that to her. But he needed her to remember, the only place he wanted to be was with her—as close as he could get.

The warm breeze brushed across his bare ass as he slipped his hand between her legs, finding her drenched. He groaned, sliding his fingers beneath her soaked folds, before using his thumb to circle her clit. She leaned her head back against the wall, trembled and moaned, circling her hips to his rhythm, moaning softly at every touch.

Until even he knew his touch was not enough. He wanted more. He wanted *everything*.

When her heated gaze met his again, telling him she wanted the same, he yanked her against him, hooking one of her legs on his arm. He hungrily took in her parted lips, while one hand stayed firmly entwined in her hair. His other held the base of his cock. "Tell me you want me," he growled.

"I want you," she whispered, her voice trembling in anticipation.

A jolt of pleasure coursed through him, and he surged forward, burying himself deep inside her in one swift stroke. Her moan echoed his and his grip on her hip tightened as their hips moved together in perfect rhythm.

Gentle wasn't what either of them wanted and with one hand tangled up in her hair, the other tight on her hip he thrust harder and faster until her eyes were scrunched shut from the pleasure radiating from within her core, and her inner walls were clenching tight around him, making him damn near cross-eyed.

Still wanting her losing herself against him, he pinned her to the wall by her hip and rocked into her harder...faster.

Harder.

Faster.

More.

Until her half-hooded eyes holding his widened as her mouth opened in a perfect O of surprise. He released all self-restraint, giving them both exactly what they craved, an explosive release that shattered them completely, and he didn't care who heard them. He pounded into her until her nails were digging into his arms and her moans were the only thing he could hear.

But then there was nothing but her coming apart as he watched on, feeling her sex clamp down like a vise until he was pumping his hips frantically, grunting his release.

When reality returned and their breathing began to slow, he trailed gentle kisses down her neck while murmuring in her ear, "Was that clear enough for you?"

She laughed softly, "Um, yes, perfectly clear."

He chuckled along with her, catching his breath, quickly helping her dress before lifting his jeans and disposing of the condom in the dumpster at the far end of the alleyway. As he returned to her, he saw her still leaning against the brick wall.

She pushed off when he reached her. "We should get back in there." As if her senses came back to her, she quickly looked around. "Do you think anyone saw that?"

"No, but they'd be lucky if they did." He grinned.

She rolled her eyes, but took his hand, leading him toward the back door. After she strode inside, he followed, sliding his cowboy hat back into place.

The moment they made it back into the bar, laughter and music filling his senses, their group regarded them closely. It was only then that Jaxon noticed her hair was a little disheveled and her cheeks were bright pink from her climax.

Eli cursed and slammed a twenty-dollar bill down on the bar.

Gunner grinned and then gave Jaxon and Charly two thumbs-up. "Thanks for making me a winner."

Charly's eyes widened. "They did not just bet that we had sex?"

Jaxon laughed, smoothing out her hair. "Seems like it." He grabbed her chin and planted a kiss on her lips. "But I'd say if anyone won here it'd be us, wouldn't you?"

Unable to resist a challenge, she grinned. "I'd say." Then said to Eli, "Next time bet on us—that's where you went wrong."

Eli tipped his hat. "Yes, ma'am."

Jaxon laughed, watching as Charly headed back behind the bar and had a quick talk with Willow and Aubrey, who began laughing, before Charly turned around again. Her gaze, satisfied and soft, met his, and he could only smile.

He had had hot sex before. But *this*, with *her*, this was an entirely different universe. And as she hit him with a smile that she didn't offer to everyone, his chest warmed in a way that told him selling his bar was the best decision he'd ever made.

Fourteen

Charly had fully intended on heading home and snuggling into her bed. That was, until Jaxon whispered in her, "Come home with me tonight. I have a surprise for you."

She couldn't deny him after that, and only wavered when she saw the ATV parked in front of his house and the excited expression on his face. "No way," she said with a firm shake of her head. "It's the middle of the night. We are *not* going out on that."

Jaxon slapped the hood in response. "It's the best time to go." Then he fished two helmets from behind the seat.

She stared at the helmet he offered. "Where exactly do you want to go?"

"I want to take you on a proper date," he said, offering her the helmet again. "Just the two of us. No distractions."

Butterflies fluttered in her belly. "You do realize, it's two o'clock in the morning."

He inclined his head. "I do, but it's a total suitable time for someone who owns a bar and has zero time to go on a date." Then he gestured at the ATV, offering her the helmet…*again.* "Come on. You'll like it. I promise."

"I'll hold you to that," she said with a little glare to add some weight to it.

He grinned in return. "I wouldn't expect any different."

She fitted the helmet over her head and he fastened the strap tight. After securing his own helmet, he opened the passenger door and Charly climbed in. He jumped in behind the wheel, and they sped away, past the barn and onto a trail leading into the night.

The engine roared, breaking the stillness of the night, and Charly grasped the metal grab bar tight. The darkness was like a blanket around the ATV, with only a glimmer of moonlight showing through the canopy of trees. The headlights of the ATV cut through the shadows, and the beams moved back and forth as Jaxon easily navigated the bends and turns.

Until the ATV slowed, and Charly spotted a tiny cottage at the end of the trail, nestled among towering trees. The stone structure was almost entirely covered with climbing ivy. Warm light spilled out through the windows, showing the two wooden rocking chairs on the porch.

Jaxon parked the ATV at the porch and cut the ignition. He moved to her as she got out and he helped her with her helmet, before removing his.

She couldn't take her eyes off the cottage. She'd never

seen anything so picture-perfect. "What is this place?" she asked.

"This cottage was my mother's most favorite place in the world," he said, smiling. "My father built this place for her when they were first married and didn't have any money."

She became lost in the warmth washing over his features— a soft look she hadn't seen from him before. "And they kept this even after they did have money?"

He nodded. "Good memories here."

"I can see why," she agreed softly. "It's breathtaking."

"Come on," he said, offering his hand. "Let me show you the rest."

She wrapped her fingers around his, and he led her to the front door. The wooden floors creaked beneath their feet as he opened it. They entered a sitting room, and she noted the plush couch with a knitted blanket along the back. A tiny galley kitchen with a small table for two by the window. A wooden ladder led up to a warm loft bedroom hidden under a sloping roof.

"This cabin is maybe the most perfect place I have ever seen in my life," she said, taking it all in with a hand pressed to her chest.

"I told you you'd like it," he said with a proud grin. "But I think I can surprise you even more." He kept her hand, leading her out a back door.

The moment she stepped outside and her eyes adjusted to the darkness, she gasped.

Tucked away between thick, tall trees and distant shadowy mountains, a hidden lake rested in the night, black glass under the reflection of the moon, which created a shimmering dance on the surface of the water. Farther above, stars shined like scattered diamonds in the sky. Just to the right, a small wooden dock jutted out into the lake, with a canoe tied to it.

Jaxon pressed a kiss against her hand before he let it go. "I get a real kick out of surprising you." He walked off to the dock.

"Where are you going?" she asked.

"For a swim," he called back over his shoulder.

She stared in amazement as he reached the end of the dock and removed his clothes, flaunting every toned muscle under the moonlight. Without hesitation, he dived into the water and resurfaced a few moments later.

"You're not scared, are you?" came his teasing voice from across the lake.

"Oh, that jerk," she mumbled beneath her breath, guessing correctly that he'd heard her reply due to the echo of his laughter.

She hurried over to where he'd undressed and shed her clothing there too, fully aware that his gaze tracked her every movement, and lingered in all the places he'd set on fire not too long ago.

Faking bravery, she jumped into the lake, resurfacing just in time to feel his strong hands drawing her closer. The water enveloped her body like a warm embrace as they swam together toward the middle of the lake. Time drifted away as they floated side by side. She let go of all her worries, responsibilities and silenced her mind.

She wasn't sure how much time had passed before Jaxon took her hand.

When she looked his way, he said, "Let's move closer to the shore."

She nodded with her mouth beneath the water and swam next to him until they reached shallow water, and soon, she was gathered in his arms, straddling his waist.

"This place is like a hidden gem," she said after a moment.

"I think that's why my mom liked it so much," he said. "It was something just for her. No one else but my mom and dad knew it existed."

She looked around, taking in the stone cottage and natural beauty surrounding them. "I can understand why it meant so much to her," she said. "It's magical here." Everything was quiet…still, like time simply didn't exist here.

"I'm happy I have it," Jaxon said with emotion in his voice. "It reminds me of them."

She wrapped her arms around his neck, holding him close. "I'm sure that would make them happy too."

Jaxon nodded, sliding up and down her back with his hands. "About tonight?" he eventually asked.

"What about it?" she asked, leaning away.

He smirked at her, locking his arms around her. "Don't get your claws out, Kitten. Just explain to me why you were so upset. It's all right to be jealous."

She shook her head. "I wasn't jealous," she muttered.

He raised an eyebrow skeptically. "What were you feeling, then?"

She didn't want to answer, but the words tumbled out of her mouth anyway. "I felt…less than her, not jealous over her."

His brows drew together tight. "Less than who?"

"Less than that woman that was hanging off you."

Awareness reached his eyes, and the softness there chipped at the coldness in her soul that felt broken. "Awe, darlin', that's a shame," he said, his hand slicing through the water before cupping her cheek. "Did Marcel cause you to feel like that?"

"His cheating made me feel that way," she admitted. "I'm sorry for my reaction. It was a knee-jerk response. I'm still getting over all the emotional baggage from all of that."

"Don't apologize for your feelings," he stated firmly. "It's understandable, given what Marcel did to you."

Smiling weakly, she leaned back in the water, wanting to return to the peacefulness found in the silence, where she felt whole and centered.

He embraced her silently, somehow understanding that she needed comfort more than words.

When she finally leaned back up to him after a long while, her hair slicked to her back from the water, she noticed the heat in his gaze from her now exposed body. But there was something more—something sweeter.

"I never would have guessed that you were a romantic,"

she said. "Bringing me here for a first date is by far the best first date—or really any date—I've ever had."

"Kitten," he said with a sly smile, "you've only seen a few of my tricks."

"Hmmm…is that so," she said playfully. "How do I get to see more of your tricks, then?"

His eyes flared. "How about another bargain?"

The water lapped around them as she paused and thought about it. "Do you think we'll ever stop challenging each other?"

"Interesting question." After taking a few moments to consider, he said, "I hope not."

She laughed a little. "Neither do I." An idea popped into her head then, and she said, "I think I can offer you something that will get you to show me a trick or two."

"Sounds tempting," he said, grinning broadly. He drew her closer, like he wanted to keep her right there with him. Then he asked teasingly, "Going to tell me what this new bargain is?"

"You show me another trick," she said, "and I'll spend the night tonight…with you."

Her words sent his eyes widening in surprise before he regained his composure, encircling her body with his arms and heading toward the shoreline.

"Where are we going now?" She laughed, gripping his waist tight with her thighs.

"I've got something waiting for us in there," he said. "Something that is sure to win you over."

"Oh?" she asked, thinking that he could not possibly top the romantic cottage and a dip in the lake. "What's that?"

A wide grin crossed his face. "A ridiculously expensive bottle of Cabernet and triple chocolate truffle cake."

Her mouth watered at the thought. "You had me at Cabernet…and you can have my soul at triple chocolate truffle cake."

He barked a laugh, striding out of the water. "You did say I am the devil after all," he said.

"Yes," she agreed. "You certainly are." And in this moment, she realized she really liked that about him too.

Fifteen

A seemingly getting-flawless month went by. The bar was becoming more popular with locals all the time, and Charly spent every night with Jaxon—sometimes together in his bed, sometimes in hers. They'd find time for dates as often as they could. She was happier now than she had ever been before, and it made her question if she'd ever felt truly fulfilled with Marcel or just accepted the life she had with him. Everything in Timber Falls was starting to come together and even Willow and Aubrey were content, often meeting up with Charly, Jaxon, Eli and Gunner when they got the opportunity.

But hanging over all that happiness with Jaxon was a feeling she couldn't shake. If she could have envisioned a dream man for herself, he was that guy. He was all the things she wanted in life from a partner: kind, strong, honorable and sexy as hell. But there was this uneasy feeling in her belly she couldn't push away.

A feeling that felt all too familiar after Marcel cheated. One that told her she wasn't enough.

She hated the way she'd reacted when she saw that woman wrap herself around Jaxon, and no matter how hard she tried, she couldn't let it go. She was never the type of woman to doubt herself and lack confidence. She hadn't when she discovered Marcel cheating with Hannah and broke things off with him. She hadn't when she uprooted her life, moving from a busy city to a small town. She hadn't when she faced every moment in her life. But that night, she had...and that sent a slice of cold fear cutting into her.

She sat on the stool at the bar, her arms resting on the top of the shiny wood, and she sighed heavily. They'd only opened the bar a half an hour ago, and the lunch rush hadn't arrived yet. Only one table was occupied, where two women sat sipping cappuccino, seemingly discussing business.

Charly wished she was talking numbers and business plans. Her head *hurt*. Her thoughts were muddled. Confusion creating a heaviness she couldn't find her way through.

She rested her chin in her hand and sighed again.

"Oh, my goodness, Charly," Aubrey grumbled. "Stop sighing and start talking about what is going on with you."

Charly blinked, suddenly reminded her best friends were in front of her getting the bar ready for the busy day ahead. The country rock playing from the speakers above the bar hit her ears again as awareness returned to her. She didn't dare sigh again, even if she wanted to. "I'm just feeling confused—that's all," she told her friends.

Willow was cutting some limes into quarters to top the drink glasses. "About Jaxon?" she asked.

A nod. "A few weeks ago when I saw that girl all over him, it made me feel so weak. Like what was happening with Marcel was happening all over again."

Aubrey gave a soft look. "I think that's expected. Marcel betrayed you terribly. Of course, when something similar happens it would bring you back to that trauma."

"I know," Charly said.

Willow stopped from adding the margarita salt into a dish and settled in front of Charly, resting her hand on Charly's arm. "But it's more than that?"

"I don't like that I don't even recognize myself," Charly said quietly, keeping the conversation private. "I don't like that I was so affected or that I jumped to immediate conclusions."

Aubrey paused from grabbing another beer to put in the fridge. She glanced up, frowning. "What do you mean?"

"I feel like I'm not emotionally stable," Charly explained, hating admitting weakness but needing her friends' input. "I'm reacting in a way that's unlike me. I don't think the worst in people immediately without proof. I'm not that person."

Willow picked up a lime and began cutting it. "But like

Aubrey said, it's kind of expected to feel shaken after what happened."

"Maybe," Charly said, before shaking her head again. "I don't know. I mean, it makes me feel…" She shoved her hands into her hair, frustration nearly blinding her. "Damaged. And that makes me think I shouldn't be even casually seeing Jaxon. The last thing I want to do is hurt Jaxon in a way that Marcel hurt me, and I don't trust myself right now and my emotions. They're all over the place."

"Whoa, girl," Aubrey said, calmly. "Maybe you should just breathe for a minute. You guys aren't serious. You're just having fun right now."

Before Charly could, a voice behind her said, "I'm really sorry to interrupt."

Charly spun on her stool, finding one of the blonde women who had to come to the last divorce party they had, who had been sitting at the table a little behind them. "You're not interrupting at all. What can I do for you?" Charly forced a professional smile.

The woman twirled the hair by her face around her finger. "I don't think you can help me, but I actually think I can help you."

Charly cocked her head. "How?"

She finally dropped her hair and sighed, crossing her arms over her chest. "We haven't met before, but I'm the assistant to the real estate agent that sold you this place."

"Billy Palmer?" Charly asked.

"That's him," she said with a nod.

Charly thought back and recalled that she did talk to this woman on numerous occasions on the telephone. "Are you Sara?" she asked.

She smiled and nodded. "Yeah, it's really nice to meet you in person."

"It's nice to meet you too," Charly said, sensing Willow and Aubrey going still behind her.

Sara's smile began to fall. "I've been hearing around town that you're seeing Jaxon Reed."

"I am," Charly confirmed.

She paused and finally glanced through her lashes, sheepishly. "Well, I kind of heard you talking about not trusting your emotions, and I know that sounds awful. I shouldn't have been eavesdropping, but I feel like it's my obligation now to tell you that Jaxon came into Billy's office after your grand opening to talk about the bar."

Charly exchanged a long look with Willow and Aubrey noting her best friends both had shock shining in their eyes. Charly's stomach immediately dropped. "To talk about the bar?" she asked.

Sara nodded. "When he had come in, he was furious that Billy would sell his bar to a bunch of women. From what I heard when I was sitting behind my desk was that he said he'd do anything to make sure you didn't ruin the bar he'd built." She paused. "I took that to mean that he'd get close to you to soften you up to what he wanted for the bar."

This wasn't exactly news to her. "We already know the locals weren't happy about us buying the bar, and honestly,

I get why they weren't. We'd completely changed the place until they didn't feel welcome."

Sara nibbled her lip. "Yeah, but it's more than that. Jaxon said that day that he wanted to buy the bar back. I know you want to see the good in him, and heck, maybe there is a lot of good in there, but he is also the same guy that would have found any way to buy you out if you hadn't done what he wanted. That's the guy he is. That's the guy he's always been."

Charly felt her blood turn cold.

Willow asked, "Are you sure you're not mistaken about what he was talking about?"

Sara shook her head. "No, I'm afraid not. I'm sorry, Charly. I wouldn't ever get involved in something like this, but I refuse to watch you get hurt when your bar is doing so much for the people in town. I'm not sure what his intentions are with you now, but I know at first, they weren't good ones." She paused. "People can change, yes, but can they change in mere weeks?" She hesitated to shrug. "I don't know."

With the room spinning around her a little, Charly swallowed her pride and her emotions crawling up her throat and nodded. "Thank you for telling me. I really appreciate you looking out for me."

Sara shrugged again. "We ladies need to look out for each other, right?"

"Yeah, we do," Charly agreed.

She sat in stunned silence, watching Sara return to the

table where her friend sat. Again, a man betrayed her, and it tasted bitter on her tongue. But more than anything, she couldn't believe she'd allowed herself to be controlled... *again*. This bar, this pact, was to pick up the pieces of their shattered lives and to build something just for them...and Jaxon wanted to steal that away to what *his* vision had been?

"Oh, Charly," Willow whispered.

She glanced toward her best friends, hating the pity on their faces, but loving them for it all the same. "It's okay," she managed to say. "Like I said, I need proof before I jump to any conclusions." She rose, sliding the stool back under the bar.

"Charly, talk to us?" Aubrey said.

Charly reached over the bar, grabbing Aubrey's arm and Willow's. "I'm all right. Honestly." She gave another forced smile. Though she knew they could read right through her, as she'd been able to read through them growing up too. "I'll be back in a few."

Neither stopped her as she left through the front door. Rain poured from the sky, a mirror image of what her heart wanted to do. She jogged down the street, not caring how soaked she got. She didn't stop running until she reached the front door of Billy's real estate office.

Out of breath, she entered the door and noted Sara's empty desk. Regardless that she hadn't made an appointment, she walked inside, strode past the desk and entered his open office.

Billy sat behind his desk and was eating a sandwich.

"Charly," he said, clearly surprised by her arrival. He set his sandwich down and wiped his mouth. "What can I do for you?"

She was sure there were a million ways to broach this, but she wasn't about to sugarcoat any of this. She needed answers. "After our grand opening the bar, did Jaxon come in here angry that the girls and I ruined his bar?"

Billy's eyebrows lifted in surprise. "I cannot talk about another client with you," he said firmly.

"Fine," Charly said. "You can blink."

Billy frowned. "I can blink?"

"Blink once if he didn't come in to see you. Blink twice if he did."

"Charly."

She crossed her arms and glared. "I have the right to know."

He blinked twice.

The ground began to feel shaky beneath her feet. "Did he suggest that he was going to do whatever he had to do to make sure I didn't ruin his bar? And if I didn't listen, he'd stop at nothing until he bought the bar back?"

She was sure she was ready for the answer, but when Billy blinked twice, she realized she wasn't ready at all, not because she didn't understand that Jaxon didn't want his bar ruined, she did understand. The tightness filling her chest came from knowing that she couldn't imagine Jaxon would ever do something so low.

"Thank you, Billy," she said, heading for the door.

"The bar meant everything to him," Billy said, coming to Jaxon's defense.

She stopped in the doorway and glanced over her shoulder, giving a smile she knew held no warmth. "I know it did. It means a lot to many people." After leaving his office, she stepped outside, lifting her head to the rain and letting it fall on her face, wishing it could wash away the emptiness filling her.

The heavy feeling weighing down her chest came from the knowledge that she couldn't believe Jaxon would do something so cruel. That wasn't the guy she knew, and *that* scared her. It reminded her that her judgement about people was off. It was off with Marcel. It was off with herself. And now she wasn't even sure if she knew Jaxon at all.

Sixteen

As the day drew to a close on the ranch, Jaxon gradually slowed his horse from a lope to a trot and eventually, to a walk. He was drenched from rain but decided to keep training regardless. Fortunately, the downpour had dissipated as he patted the young horse. The air was filled with an array of earthy aromas, the pleasant smell of damp soil, followed by the sweet aroma of flowers and grasses after the thunderstorm. Droplets of rain had left puddles across the land.

He steered the horse toward the gate of the sand ring and opened it before guiding her out and closing it again. The little mare was calmer now after a hard ride, and she stopped fighting against his aids.

Instead of returning to the barn, he took the little mare down the driveway along the grassy side to cool her off. She spooked at a boulder as she passed beneath an old pine tree, so he spent some time walking back and forth until she regained composure despite all the imaginable scary things that lurked around them.

As they headed back up the driveway, he took out his cell from his pocket—he'd texted Charly three times today but hadn't received any response nor did she answer when he called twice.

He couldn't shake off his worry. Though he knew if something happened to Charly, Willow or Aubrey would have been sure to contact him.

By the time he returned to barn, the little mare wasn't breathing heavily anymore, having cooled off quite nicely. Though as they neared her paddock, she threw her head back and forth, tail swishing excitedly.

Jaxon chuckled. He loved a good spicy mare.

"Great ride?" Decker asked as he approached him near the barn.

"Yeah, she was fantastic." He took a minute to pat the mare, dismounted, and pulled the reins over her head. "She's got potential, just needs a little more work." The slow gates of this mare made her perfect for the western hunter show ring. But some needed more time to train than others, and she was one of them. Mares weren't always easily won over; trust was earned with most of them, not given. He just hadn't gotten there yet, but he would. He always did.

"That's it for me today," he said to Wayne, as he strode out of the barn.

Wayne nodded. "Got it, boss. See you tomorrow." He

strode off with the mare to hose her off before putting her back out to pasture.

Decker asked, "Is there anything you want me to do before I leave?"

Turning back to him, Jaxon shook his head, unzipping his chaps. "We're good. See you tomorrow."

"Have a good night," Decker called, walking toward his truck in the driveway.

Before calling it a day, Jaxon deposited his chaps in the barn and then headed toward Gunner and Eli who were leaning against the fence of the paddock holding the new two-year-old horses that they'd brought up from the roundup. He noticed that they were just as drenched as he was. "How did it go?" he asked, sliding next to them.

They'd spent all day continuing handling these young horses by doing some groundwork with them to get them used to human interaction. Not an easy task as most of these horses had minimal interaction with humans before.

"We had a good day overall except for one," Gunner said.

Jaxon scanned the horses, found a dark bay horse with a white star on its forehead staring right at him challengingly as though daring him to move forward. He chuckled at how fierce that horse looked, reminded him of another set of fiery eyes—Charly's eyes. He wanted to go to Charly immediately to find out what was going on, but he lived by his father's rule: *never leave a horse insecure.*

His father believed in natural horsemanship and the idea

of building a connection, not fear. Jaxon respected and lived by the same methods.

"No luck yet with her?" Jaxon asked, resting a boot on the bottom of the fence.

Eli shook his head. "Not even close."

Jaxon pulled away from the fence and opened the gate, causing the young horses to scatter—all except for the mare who stood still, eyes focused on him. Every year, they had at least one horse that was different from the others: alert and observant, instead of running away in flight mode like the rest. Every horse was a gift, but some were simply smarter and more aware than others.

He respected that strength. He wouldn't break it by beating the horse into submission like he had seen done before.

With confidence yet gentleness, he approached the horse, but stopped when a few feet remained between them. The horse snorted at him, standing tall with its ears perked forward, declaring him the enemy.

Time slowly passed as Jaxon gently advanced closer with an outstretched arm. Five minutes…ten minutes…twenty minutes…

Jaxon breathed in deeply and exhaled slowly, calming himself. He held eye contact with the horse and kept his hand held out, even though his arm ached from holding it still for so long.

The minutes ticked by, but Jaxon remained patient, waiting until the horse stretched its neck and gave his hand a sniff. He slowly pulled away but couldn't help but smile at the horse's reaction. "Not so bad am I, sweetie?" he asked as the horse looked at him with softer eyes this time. "You just wait, we'll be friends before you know it." After leaving the mare better than he found her, Jaxon headed toward the gate.

Eli scoffed as he locked it behind him. "It's annoying how easy you make that look," he commented.

Jaxon chuckled. "What can I say? Everyone loves my charm."

Eli snorted.

Gunner barked a loud laugh. Until his laughter faded. "Are we still on for tonight with the girls?" he asked.

Good question. Jaxon shrugged. "I need to go see Charly. She's not answering my calls. I'll let you know."

Eli lifted a knowing brow at him. "What did you do?" he asked.

"Why do you think it's something I did?" Jaxon retorted.

"Because we know you," Gunner replied with a shrug.

Jaxon snorted. Even if he knew they were right that he often made a mess of things without even trying sometimes, he didn't want to admit it. He said goodbye to them and left for his truck.

Driving down empty roads and scenic routes, Jaxon couldn't help but wonder what he had done to upset Charly enough to ignore him all day. He had a feeling he wasn't going to like the answer.

When he finally pulled into downtown, luck was on his side with a parking spot not far from the bar and he parked at the curb. Exiting his truck, he was met with a bouquet of scents. He could smell the coffee emanating from the nearby café and the aroma of freshly baked bread from the local bakery. He waved at the locals he passed, soon entering through the bar's front door.

He felt like he was walking straight into positive energy and a sense of empowerment as '90s music played through the speakers. Throughout the crowded bar, he found celebrating women and a banner that read: Divorced AF, and Jaxon immediately understood he was in for a stormy night ahead. Every single woman looked his way like he was the enemy. And to them, he probably was.

Though nothing could have prepared him for when he reached the bar, finding Willow and Aubrey behind it.

Both were glaring at him, and not like the other women there. This felt personal. "Where's Charly?"

"Busy," Aubrey said. "Go away."

He bristled and looked to Willow, only to find her glaring daggers at him now. "Willow—"

"Don't Willow me," she snapped, folding her arms across her chest. "What is wrong with you?"

He frowned. "What exactly have I done?"

Aubrey looked on the verge of throwing something at him. She placed her hands on her hips and snarled, "Do we really have to explain it to you?"

Jaxon glanced between the two, feeling like he'd entered a combat zone. "I've tried calling and texting Charly all day, but she hasn't responded and I came to talk to her," he explained. Was that what had them ready to send him out to the sharks?

Willow scoffed, while Aubrey propped her hands on the bar and scowled at him.

"Does this sound familiar?" Aubrey said venomously. "Oh, Billy—how could you sell my bar to these women without telling me of their plan? How can I buy the bar back if I can't weasel my way into one of their hearts to get her to change her vision? You're so slimy, Jaxon Reed."

Willow nodded in agreement.

Jaxon took in every word, feeling like each one was a smack to his face. He remembered that day. He'd been angry after realizing the bar he'd built was being turned into something not fit for the town. "It wasn't like that," he said gently. "I had my back up then when I first came into the bar. I didn't know any of you."

"Is that supposed to make this better?" Willow asked.

Jaxon cringed. "No, I guess it doesn't."

Right at that moment, the door to the back room opened and Charly stepped out carrying a box of craft beer. When she spotted Jaxon, she barely registered he stood there. Without even acknowledging him, she placed the box on the bar top and quickly turned away to return to the back room.

"Charly," he called over the music, desperation now tearing through his chest.

She stopped, visibly sighed and slowly turned around.

"I can't talk now. I'll come by your place after I'm done tonight."

The loud voices, the god-awful music, it all faded around him as his world narrowed on her. He moved closer to her, wanting to take her in his arms and beg for forgiveness. "Please let me explain…"

But before he could finish, she backed away from him and shut her eyes tightly. When she opened them again, she wore a stone-cold expression. "We need to talk, Jaxon, but not now and not here. Please do as I say and leave. I'll come to your house later."

Jaxon felt himself nodding numbly, but what he really wanted was to remain there and plead his case. He kept his mouth shut though, knowing he needed to think this through before he said something to make it even worse.

He turned, catching Willow and Aubrey still glaring at him. "I just need to explain," he told them, sure that she'd understand where he had been coming from.

Aubrey glanced at Willow and then narrowed her eyes on Jaxon. "I think you've done enough talking, don't you?"

His reply died on his tongue.

The walls seemed to be shrinking in on him as his shame sapped the air from the room. He knew that not only did he have to make things right with Charly, but also with Willow and Aubrey. "I'll set this straight with her," he vowed, as he marched toward the door, not sure how he would undo the damage that had been done.

Seventeen

Charly's eyelids felt heavy as she navigated the curvy two-lane road, leaving Willow and Aubrey to close the bar. The divorce party for the woman who came from a bigger city to the West was a smashing success. Word of the bar was getting out there, and Charly was glad for it. More locals were coming in and everyone looked like they were right at home. Gone were miserable faces, replaced by people having fun. But she felt like someone cracked her head open and scrambled the inside. She'd wanted to kick Jaxon where it hurt for what he'd said to Billy, but as the day had passed after talking to Sara, her anger had dissipated.

Now, without the fury, all that was left was soul-deep exhaustion.

The drive to Jaxon's place was much too quick, considering she had no idea what to say to him. Being angry had been easy. Whatever this feeling was nearly strangling her was so much more complicated.

When she drove up the driveway, lights on either side of her car guided her up. The ranch was bathed in darkness, minus the bright light on the outside of the door and the porch light. But even with just those, she found Jaxon quickly. He was sitting on the porch steps, like he'd been there all along, waiting for her arrival.

Her car came to a stop next to his truck and she took a few deep breaths, trying to muster her courage for the difficult conversation ahead. She wasn't sure if what she was doing was the right thing, her heart full of uncertainty and apprehension, but there was no backing out now.

Jaxon tracked her with his eyes the whole time she moved to him. A combination of worry and shame weighed heavily on his face, and it seemed like he was just as uncomfortable as she was.

Good. She wanted him to sit in that discomfort a little. She'd been sitting it in all damn day.

The soft hooting of an owl in the distance was all that disturbed the peace of the night. The horses nearby grazed, their dark figures standing out against the silvery light of the moon.

Finally, standing next to him, she broke the thick silence that hung between them, and said, "Hey."

"Hey," he replied softly.

She waited for all the things she wanted—needed—to say to come spilling out of her mouth, but nothing came.

In the heavy silence, Jaxon heaved a long sigh. "Please let me explain."

"You don't owe me anything," Charly told him wearily, taking a seat next to him on the porch steps. "You don't even owe me an explanation."

"Like hell I don't—I obviously hurt you," he argued fiercely. He took her hand in his, holding tight. "Please just listen to me."

She stared into his eyes for a moment before speaking. "What do you need to say?"

"I get why this looks bad," he said, voice rough. "I'm ashamed of how I felt when you first took over the bar. I never should have gone to Billy. I never should have said that I wanted to buy the bar back. It truly was less about *you*, and more about how the bar I built was changing into something I wasn't ready for."

"Don't be ashamed," she said. As much as she wanted to yell at him, she felt like she had a pretty good feel of who Jaxon was as a man. "I know giving up the bar wasn't your choice. I also know what the bar meant to you. I get that. I understand that watching it being taken over and ripped apart must have been hard for you. I'm not mad about it."

He arched a questioning eyebrow at her. "You're not mad about it?"

"Well, I was mad about it, believe me," she corrected with a soft laugh. "I thought I'd come here livid, saying all sorts of things that would hurt you. Because that's how I felt when I heard what you said to Billy. But really, after calming down, I realized that I can't fault you for being upset at what we'd done to the bar and desperately trying to find a way to save what you had built. We had dismantled your bar that you loved, and we'd pissed off a lot of the locals in the process." She squeezed his hand in return, feeling a peaceful contentment settle over her in her decision. "The bar is better now because of you, and I'm grateful for that. That's why I'm here—to tell you that you don't owe me anything. We were both doing the same thing—trying to save the bar in the way we saw fit, and I probably would have acted the same as you had if the roles were reversed."

"That isn't true, Charly," he said with conviction. "We aren't the same. You are better than me. You're incredible."

Warmth spread throughout her chest, but she couldn't even bring herself to smile. Deep down she just felt exposed and raw.

He dropped his chin, staring down at their held hands. "You're really not mad at me?"

"I'm really not mad at you," she said.

"Good," he breathed, slowly shaking his head. "I'm so damn relieved. I thought I blew this." He lifted his hand to reach for her face and went to lean in.

She pulled away, staying out of his reach. "You didn't blow anything, but I can't do this anymore."

He frowned, slowly lowering his hand. "I thought you said you weren't angry."

"I'm not angry at you," she agreed. "But through all this, I've just realized that I'm not ready for a relationship.

I never should have let this happen." Her heart bled at this realization. That even if Jaxon was a good thing, she was too emotionally damaged to even let that happiness in. For herself, she felt sad. "Honestly, I don't even think I'm over the last one I was in."

His hand tightened around hers, and she saw the shift in his expression, the relief that had been there fading fast. "We don't have to rush anything. We don't even have to label it. Can we not just continue getting to know each other?"

She shook her head firmly. "No, because now that I see the hot emotional mess I am, I can't unsee it. I need to figure myself out again. I need to find my way back to the woman I was before Marcel's betrayal, and I can't do that with you there." She paused, drew in a shaky breath before continuing, "When I moved here, I promised myself that my focus would be on the bar, to see it succeed, to make it something the girls and I would be proud of. And somewhere along the line, I forgot what I wanted."

He cocked his head, rubbing his thumb over her hand. "You can still have all of that with me at your side."

Part of her wished she could believe him, but that part was the part of her that always ended up getting hurt. "That's where you're wrong," she replied softly. "I need to focus on me without a relationship getting in the way." She released his hand and added, "I feel fragile...vulnerable... and I can't trust my own emotions or that you're fully who you say you are, and that's not fair to either of us."

He hesitated, and she wondered if he wouldn't own it.

Though he surprised her, and offered, "I was that ass who went to Billy in fear that my bar was being ruined," he said. "I was also that guy who thought he could win you over and get you to see where you went wrong. But I'm also the guy who changed after spending time with you."

She wasn't even sure why she was indulging him. Her mind was made up. She needed to go back to plan A: *focus on her bar, not on a cowboy.* But the question rolled off her tongue. "How did you change?" she asked.

His gaze lifted to hers and held. "I wanted you to succeed." His voice was barely a whisper now. "I still want that."

Her heart squeezed tight, wanting so desperately to soften for him. "Thank you for being honest, and for wanting that for me."

The air around them felt heavy with tension.

Until he broke the silence, then an uncomfortable sadness drifted in between them. "I'm sorry, Charly, so damn sorry for hurting you, and for being such an asshole."

"You weren't an asshole," she told him. "You were fighting for something you worked hard for, and honestly, I understand that."

His gaze held depth that she wanted to cling to. "This doesn't have to be the end of us," he said gently.

"I'm afraid it does," she told him firmly. "All this just reminded me I'm not ready for anything this serious, where I care if another woman is in your arms. After what I went through with Marcel, I want fun. I want laughter. I don't want a broken heart. Especially when I feel like my heart is so raw a very little thing could break it." To put this conversation to bed for good, she said, "You know how you felt when you gave up your bar for your dad—that you had a duty to see something through. That's how this feels to me. I need to stay focused. I can't do this with my emotions all over the place, and they are when I'm with you."

The tenderness in his gaze once would have weakened her resolve, but not tonight; things had shifted between them too much. She rose and began to back away from him, taking a couple steps down the porch steps. "I'm sorry that I can't continue this," she told him quietly, "and I'm sorry if my actions led you on in any way."

Jaxon's arms trembled as if he was fighting against jumping up and taking her back into his arms. He shook his head firmly. "You've never misled me," he insisted softly. "If there is any fault here, it's all on me."

He finally rose and stepped closer to her and embraced her one last time. She both hated and loved how much comfort she found in his arms.

Her eyes shut as he pressed a gentle kiss to her forehead. "I want to use the wish you owe me," she said, taking a step away off the porch steps.

He shoved his hands into his pockets. His voice rough. "Name it."

"That you'll stay my friend."

He went statue still, before his expression softened. "You'll always have a friend in me, Charly."

"Good, I'm glad." She smiled in return, before forcing herself to move away, no matter how right it felt being in his arms. Her emotions swirled around her, a mix of sadness and confusion, but she headed for her car before she talked herself into going straight back into his arms.

He stared pleadingly at her like that's exactly where he wanted her to go.

Not again. Never again.

She could never forget again that she had to come first. Her dreams mattered. She was building a new life for herself, and she needed to build that life before opening her heart again.

"Goodbye, Jaxon," she called before getting into her car. She didn't hear his reply past the rapid beat of her heart rate in her ears. But as she drove off, she saw his shadowy figure in the rearview mirror. She knew she was making the right decision, despite her heart begging her to go back.

Eighteen

The flames from the fire Jaxon had built crackled as he perched on the log, the mountains at his back, surrounded by thick evergreen trees. The silence of the wilderness enveloped him with the air carrying a hint of pine scent that mingled with the scent of the campfire's burning logs. Tonight's plan for a night with Charly was long gone now. This very location had been the hot spot during his teenage years. It was the perfect place to hook up, when he held parties with a bonfire and did too much underage drinking, but now, in his thirties, he came here for the quiet.

As he sat, Thunder chomping on the grass behind him, tied to a tree, Jaxon felt the legend of the wilderness surround him: *I brought her to you...and you threw her away.*

Feeling like he'd failed in every which way, Jaxon leaned forward over his knees, elbows resting on his legs, hands rubbing his face. Everything Charly had said played back in his mind like an old movie reel he couldn't stop.

He was struggling to fix his mistake, to repair the broken trust between himself and Charly. She'd said she wasn't ready for a relationship, but he knew it went far beyond that. She simply didn't want to deal with any bullshit—and he'd given her a whole shovel's worth. If he had told her what he'd said to Billy long before now, and explained himself then, they would have been having a great night and she'd be enveloped in his arms.

For such a long time, he'd lived life carelessly, doing as he pleased and never really considering anyone else's feelings or opinions. He'd built his bar on his terms. He'd put his professional goals ahead of his personal life. Now all that was essential for him was making amends with Charly.

She didn't want anything to do with him anymore... and for good reason. But he wanted to find a way to show her life was better with him there. That he wasn't an anchor that would drown her, but he was there to stand by her while she floated up to her dreams.

For so long, he'd only thought of himself. He hadn't truly cared what anyone thought of him. Until Charly.

He cursed and thrust his hands into his hair. His father would be ashamed of him, and so would his mother. The one thing he'd learned from them was the value of family. He saw that not only in how they raised him, but also in the way his father ran the ranch and treated the cowboys. Choosing his professional life over the importance of a personal life had led him to a bar he no longer owned, and a woman that he wanted to keep in his life, who didn't want anything to do with him.

His choices led him to this. His ego for having his bar changed destroyed any chance he had with Charly. Shame dripped into every pore of his body.

Before long, the sound of thundering hooves made him turn his head toward the noise. Sure enough, Gunner and Eli were riding toward him.

When they reached him, Jaxon could barely look them in the eye. "How'd you know I was here?" he asked.

"Decker saw you head out and called," said Eli, as he and Gunner hopped off their horses. They tied them up next to Thunder and joined him around the fire.

Damn, he must have looked worse than he thought if Decker sent out reinforcements.

Eli pulled a flask from his jacket, offering it to Jaxon. "Thought you might need this."

"You have no idea. Thanks." Jaxon accepted it gratefully and downed a big swig of burning whiskey. He grimaced as it went down his throat.

"Want to tell us what's going on?" Eli asked.

Gunner and Eli had known Jaxon since he was a little kid. They'd gone through all the years of school together. They'd been through big highs and terrible lows. But *this*... Jaxon had never gone through this—he'd always been in control, not needing anyone...

He sighed, rubbing the spot on his chest that wouldn't

stop aching. After taking another shot, he handed the flask to Gunner and gave them a recap that Charly had found out he went to Billy and suggested buying the bar back if he couldn't change their minds on the vision for the bar.

"Ouch," Gunner said before taking his own swig from the flask.

"You could say that," Jaxon agreed, rubbing the back of his aching neck. "She handled it better than I would have expected…which somehow made it worse." The embers of the campfire flew up into the night sky as he continued, "I thought I could handle her coming over to my house and giving me a piece of her mind. Instead, she said she understood why I did what I did because she would have done anything to save her bar too."

Eli frowned. "Isn't that a good thing?"

He closed his eyes briefly before replying in a strained voice, "Regardless how she felt about it, and that she ultimately forgave me for being an ass, it's over and there's nothing I can do about that."

"Anything can be worked out," Eli offered.

Jaxon shook his head, holding out his hand for the flash again. Once Gunner handed it to him, he took another long swig. "I don't think so. This just reminded her of her heartbreak she's been through. That she once planned a life with a man who destroyed those plans, no less than three months ago. I reminded her that a relationship can hurt." He ran his hands through his hair and let out a deep breath.

"She wanted out and I don't blame her. There's a reason relationships are hard—and why I avoided them."

"You don't mean that," Gunner said, with a stern face. "Those were empty days, Jaxon, and lonely nights—you don't want to do that again. These past weeks with Charly were the happiest I've ever seen you."

"Agreed," Eli said.

They were right, Jaxon felt that truth right down to his gut, but the pressure still weighed heavily on Jaxon's shoulders. He shouldn't have gone to Billy all for his own ego. What had he been thinking? His behavior with women would never have made his parents proud. No doubt they had wanted him to find a woman just like Charly to settle down with and give them grandchildren. Now karma was reaping its revenge on him. Because he liked Charly.

Spending time with her and her friends made him realize he wanted to be a better man. He wanted to be a man that others looked up to. He wanted women to think highly of him. And the thought of not hearing Charly laugh, not seeing that smile, not feeling her melt beneath his hands, was a punishment he did not want to endure.

"Was that the only reason?" Gunner asked, as if that wasn't enough of one.

Jaxon sighed, scrapping a hand over his tired eyes. "She wants to focus on the bar and put all her effort there." He dropped his hands, looking between his friends. "Putting her professional life before her personal life—ever heard that before?"

Eli's mouth twitched. "Sounds familiar."

Jaxon had done that his whole life too. It felt like some twisted joke that the logic he used for not wanting a relationship was now smacking him in the face when he wanted to get serious with someone.

Jaxon handed Eli the flask, as Eli asked, "How did she find out about your conversation with Billy anyway?"

He shrugged. "No clue, but given everything, I suspect it was likely someone looking out for her worried that she was going to get hurt."

Neither friend commented on that, but Gunner chimed in, "Everything can be fixed. What you did isn't unforgivable."

"She's already forgiven me for it," Jaxon retorted. "The bigger problem is that I reminded her of all the reasons she originally thought I was trouble. I reminded her that somehow, she forgot a relationship shouldn't be her focus."

Eli snorted, giving Jaxon a *look*. "So, you're just going to sit here and mope?"

"Nope," Jaxon replied, taking the flask from Eli again. "I'm going to sit here and get drunk."

Gunner grinned then pulled out two more flasks from his pocket. "Good thing I brought more."

"Perfect," Jaxon said, before throwing back another shot. His stomach was warm and throat on fire but numb felt better than what he'd been feeling before.

"Well, if any good came of this," Gunner said, "you got

what you set out to do. The bar is in good shape. Everyone in town is thrilled, and so are the cowboys."

The fire crackled as Eli added, "Not only that, but Willow and Aubrey seem happy too. The bar is finally busy again. Every time I go in there for lunch, it's packed full. I would take that as a win."

Jaxon bit back a curse. He shook his head, adamant. "I'm happy for them, but there is no winning here. The woman I want is done with me."

The urge to run after her was strong, but Jaxon knew he had no right to interfere in Charly's decision. She'd been through a lot...too much. He would not add to her misery. All his will and strength kept him rooted to the spot instead of jumping back on Thunder and riding off to beg her to give him another chance.

"Haven't you ever listened to any of my songs?" Gunner asked with a bite to his voice. "Every love story is about a love worth fighting for. Maybe this is your time to make some real changes and fight for something meaningful."

"That's great and all," Jaxon said, dryly. He picked up a stick and began poking at the red-hot coals. "But I don't even know where to start."

Eli gave a dry chuckle. "Fortunately, Charly is smarter than you are. If anyone can figure out how to heal her broken heart, it's probably her. Why don't you just ask her how you can make this right?"

"Because she didn't give me that chance," he answered flatly. "It's done."

Sitting by the fire, gazing up at the sparks flying up into the night sky, his friends made it sound so simplistic, yet nothing about this felt easy.

"I said that I'd still be her friend," he growled, wishing he could erase those words he'd said. "Why the hell would I say that? I should have said something better…" He should have said *stay*. He should have fought harder.

Eli lifted his brows. "You friend zoned yourself?"

The warmth of the fire embraced Jaxon as the chill of his reality stormed across him. "Yes," he grumbled.

"Well, we all know why you did that," Gunner said, an orange hue from the flames casting a warm glow across his knowing gaze.

Jaxon arched an eyebrow. "Care to fill me in."

Gunner grinned. "You're an idiot."

Eli just shrugged. "He's not wrong."

Even Jaxon couldn't argue, though it didn't get him any closer to making this right with Charly.

Nineteen

The next morning, Charly awoke to beams of sunlight streaming through her bedroom window. With a groan, she pulled the pillow over her head, ready to hibernate for another day. Nothing felt right this morning, and shouldn't it have? She'd done the logical thing. She needed to focus on herself and her dreams, before letting someone else in. And that someone needed to be damn near perfect. Jaxon's red flag had popped up its ugly head and she couldn't ignore that.

She would never ignore any red flags again. No matter that her heart kept telling her she'd made a huge mistake. Her heart was screaming at her that even if Jaxon went to Billy and clearly didn't have the best intentions then, once he got to know her, he had changed. Even she hadn't had the best intentions in the beginning, which was why forgiving him was so easy.

But her head refused to listen. She'd done this all before…
and had been burned in the end, leaving her with nothing.
She needed to build her life, on her own, before opening
her heart again.

Unfortunately for her, she didn't get the chance to hide
away from the world forever. Before she knew it, her bedroom door swung open and Willow and Aubrey tiptoed in,
debating whether they should wake her up.

Charly groaned, "I'm already awake."

"Good. Get up," Aubrey said, "We've made breakfast
for you."

Charly just grumbled in response, pressing the pillow
tighter around her head. "Go away. I'm not going anywhere today."

This *was* the right decision. This made sense. Staying
clear of him was her only choice.

But why did that feel like the wrong choice? Why did
she feel like she was missing something this morning? She
thought she'd wake up feeling like finally everything was
back in order. She had a plan. She had a vision…and none
of it made her feel happy.

When she didn't move the pillow away, Willow *tsked* and
chided softly, "You can't hide away in here all day."

"Oh, yeah?" Charly argued, "Just watch me."

She felt the bed dip as Willow sat down in exasperation.
"Well, you better talk it out, because if you don't, it's going
to bug you all day."

"I don't even know what I'm feeling after last night,"

Charly admitted, feeling like her heart and head were torn in opposite directions. She sought peace and contentment, and this was the exact opposite of that. "I did the right thing but why do I feel so miserable?"

"Because you like him," Aubrey offered without the usual snark to her voice.

Charly huffed against the pillow pressed to her nose. "I don't want to like him. I want to focus on the bar, make a huge success and not think about a boyfriend."

Suddenly the pillow was yanked away, and Aubrey was staring at her with a knowing look. "Hate to break it to you, but you do like him. A lot, even. Because the fact that you didn't murder him last night tells me that you care about him more than you're letting yourself believe," she said sharply.

"Fine," Charly admitted, squinting her eyes against the bright sun. "I do care about him, but he shouldn't be so hard to walk away from. He wanted to buy the bar back! He got close to me, knowing that if we didn't listen, he planned to do what he could to get the bar out of our hands."

"Yeah, well people change," Willow commented, taking a seat next to Charly. "Maybe Jaxon isn't the same person he was when we first arrived here. Maybe he saw something in you that makes him want to do better. Maybe you shouldn't write him off so fast."

Aubrey gave a small shrug. "I know we've changed a lot since we've all been here. I don't think it's fair for you to blame him for wanting to protect his bar."

"I'm not blaming him for wanting to protect his bar," countered Charly, "It's just complicated. It's like when everything happened with Marcel, I felt so embarrassed that I didn't see it coming or know any better, and I promised myself it would never happen again...then I met Jaxon. Now I just feel foolish all over again. I feel like I'm about to repeat the same mistakes, and I haven't been single that long. This is all too much, too fast, and I feel like a step away from emotionally unraveling, when I should be focusing on putting all the pieces back together." She placed the pillow firmly back over her face. "I don't want to think about it...about a guy."

"That's probably not possible now, babe," Aubrey said. "You're going to have to deal with this. And, from what I've seen of Jaxon, I don't think he's just going to let you walk away."

"He did last night," she mumbled beneath the pillow.

Willow gave a soft snort, taking the pillow away again and setting it aside. "Did you even give him a chance to do otherwise?"

"No," Charly said, staring up at her ceiling fan rhythmically spinning. "Should I have?"

"Only you can answer that," Aubrey said. Then added, "But yes."

Charly groaned, glancing at her best friends. Everyone needed someone in their corner that told it to them straight, and Charly had always been grateful for her friends. "Is that so?"

Aubrey nodded. "You've been really happy with him."

"And you can't deny that," Willow agreed.

Charly glanced between her friends and sighed. "Are you telling me I shouldn't have ended it, even after all I've said this morning?"

"I'm not saying that," Willow said with a little shrug. "I'm just saying that he's not the same guy we first met, and maybe you shouldn't hold it against him. No one is perfect."

"And," Aubrey added, "he's been good to you ever since that day...and yes, he made you unbelievably happy. Happier than I ever saw you with Marcel."

Charly huffed, glancing up at her ceiling fan again. Was she expecting too much? No, she didn't think so. What he'd done landed him in the jerk zone and she needed to protect herself. But he had apologized and meant it—she believed that. "Maybe—" Her phone rang on her bedside table. She snatched it up and checked the caller ID. Her heart sank when it was an unknown number, not Jaxon. "Hello?" she said into the phone.

A sweet female voice spoke on the other end of the line. "Hello," she said, "is this Miss Charly Henwood?"

"Yes," she replied reluctantly. Great. Now she had to deal with a spam call.

"Hi, Miss. Henwood, this is Dr. Leo from Arizona General Hospital," the doctor said. Charly's heart now skipped a beat, a thousand thoughts racing through her mind all at once. "Do you know Marcel Boucher?"

It took her a second to absorb her question. "Yes," she responded in almost a whisper. "He's my ex-fiancé."

"I see," the doctor said softly. "We have your name listed as his next of kin."

"What's happened?" she managed to ask. "Is he okay?"

"Unfortunately, Mr. Boucher was in a bad car accident last night. His car collided with a transport truck after a drunk driver blew through an intersection. He came into the ER around three o'clock in the morning."

Charly held her breath, feeling like she was floating. There, but not there. "Is he seriously injured?" she asked, not sure she wanted to know the answer.

"It is gravely serious, I'm afraid," the doctor advised. "I suggest you contact his family and get to the hospital quickly."

Charly swallowed against the emotion tightening her throat, trying to make her mind work. "Yes… I can call his sister, but she is in France right now." She thought back to Marcel's parents' travel plans. They had always been wanderers, traveling all over the world. "I believe his parents are on a cruise around the Mediterranean."

"It is important you get his family here," the doctor said. She paused, hinting at what Charly didn't want to hear: *Marcel was dying.*

"I'm in Montana right now," Charly told the doctor. "But I'll be on the first plane to Phoenix." Her voice caught in her throat as she mustered up the courage to ask, "Is he going to make it?"

The doctor's pause answered her question: *no.* "He will have as much time as we need for you and his family to get here," she explained gently. "He is currently intubated and on life support. I'll see you when you arrive." The line went dead after that.

Charly made an unfamiliar noise deep in her chest, anguish cutting through her heart with an intensity that she couldn't control. She didn't know if she should scream, cry or do both. She was supposed to forget Marcel and move on, and it felt like some sick joke that her heart and strength was being tested even further.

"What is it?" Willow asked when Charly dropped her phone onto the bed with shaky hands.

She could barely choke out the words. "Marcel…he was in a bad car accident."

"Is he okay?" Aubrey asked, her voice trembling.

Charly shook her head slowly and replied, "He's on life support. I—I don't think he's going to make it." Her strength began to sway with this truth and her friends wrapped their arms around her in a hug. They were murmuring words of comfort, but all she could make out was herself saying, "I wished for this to happen. I did this."

Willow leaned away from Charly, taking her hands in hers. "You didn't want this to happen," she said firmly. "What are you talking about?"

Charly's breath hitched, her welling eyes spilling over. "I wanted him to hurt. I wanted him to suffer for what he did to me. I made this happen."

Aubrey interrupted with a sharp voice. "Stop it! You couldn't have made this happen. It was just a car accident. This is not about you. Don't put that on yourself."

But why did it feel like it was? Why did it feel like she had somehow brought this fate onto him?

Charly felt her whole being break apart. She had been so ready to let go of the past hours ago...until now realizing that past would be gone forever. With jelly legs and panic coursing through her veins, she pushed the blanket off her body and slid out of bed.

"I need to go," she muttered while grabbing her cell phone. "Please help me get a flight ticket. I need to leave as soon as possible."

Willow took Charly's cell out of her hands, nodding in agreement. "I'll find you a flight, go pack."

Aubrey rushed into the closet saying, "I'll help you."

Charly barely felt the ground under feet as she moved absentmindedly and pulled out clothes from her drawers with shaking hands. She'd wanted to say goodbye to Marcel for closure and to put him behind her, but she wasn't ready to say goodbye forever.

Twenty

The day had come and gone, and Jaxon was losing his damn mind. Less than twenty hours had gone by since he last saw Charly, yet he felt like he was going to explode. He'd spent his entire life without her, and now he wasn't sure how he could spend another minute without her near him. It didn't make sense. He'd never needed anyone this bad—but he needed her.

He'd ridden two horses this morning and both hadn't gone well. Likely also due to his wicked hangover. His head was not in the game. He couldn't remember the last time in his life when he was so indecisive. He usually knew how to manage things and what he wanted, but now he was running his hands through his hair, pacing along the front of his house, while spitting out every curse word in his vocabulary.

"What's he doing?" Gunner asked, as Jaxon paced in front of the steps leading up to his porch.

Leaning against his truck, Eli replied, "Having a possible breakdown."

Settling in next to Eli, Gunner called, "Are you having a breakdown?"

Jaxon froze on the spot, directed his gaze at them and scowled. Everyone was working around him at the farm, but he'd barely said a word to anyone all day. And eventually everyone stopped talking to him.

The sun remained hidden behind a thick blanket of gray clouds, matching his mood. The air felt heavy and damp, as if the weight of the clouds pressed down upon his shoulders. He pushed past it all, searching for the warmth and the light. "I can't let her go," he finally said aloud.

No one spoke up after he declared this, so he turned back to face his childhood friends. "How do I win her over again?" His voice was near begging. The sensation he felt burning through his veins was unbearable. If he had to endure this much longer, he'd crawl out of his damn skin.

Eli shook his head doubtfully. "You're asking the wrong person for advice about love. I'm horrible at relationships."

Jaxon looked at Gunner for an answer. "You write songs about love," he said. Hopefully Gunner knew some secret Jaxon didn't. "What should I do? Drop to my knees and grovel, begging for forgiveness?"

Gunner raised his hands as if surrendering and shrugged. "Just because I write songs about love doesn't mean that I actually know anything about it. Most of my inspiration comes from other people. It's not personal."

Jaxon swore angrily once more continuing to pace.

Charly had made it clear that she didn't want any kind of relationship with him now, and he understood. She'd just come off a heartbreak. The last thing she'd want was complicated, and because of his talk with Billy, Jaxon had made it complicated. "I have no idea how to change her mind," he called out, frustration clenching his jaw.

Eli cleared his throat and offered, "Just an idea, but if there's anyone who knows what you should do, I suspect it would be her two best friends."

Jaxon stopped pacing and considered it. He shoved his hands into his pockets. "Would talking to them cross a line?" The last thing he wanted to do was piss Charly off more.

Gunner shrugged again nonchalantly and suggested, "I don't think so. You're asking for advice, what's the harm in that. Besides, it's probably the best way to get an answer anyway. They know her. They'll know if you should back off and stay away, or if you can somehow fix this."

Jaxon pondered, thinking it all through, but the same thought came slamming back into his mind. He couldn't accept Charly's refusal of a relationship. Nothing seemed right without her. He'd never fought for anything this hard before besides his bar, and he wanted to fight for her.

Done with standing around and doing nothing to make this right, he grabbed his phone out of his pocket and searched for the bar's new number and dialed it.

After three rings, Willow answered with her gentle voice, "The Naked Moose."

"Hey Willow, it's Jaxon," he said, hoping to hell this

didn't backfire on him. "Is Charly at the bar with you right now?"

She hesitated before replying, "No, she isn't here right now."

"That's what I was hoping for," said Jaxon, only imagining the confusion Willow must feel at such a statement. "Listen, can I drive over and talk to you and Aubrey?"

"Ah…" Willow paused, and her voice became muffled, telling him she was talking to Aubrey. She finally said, "Yeah sure, come on by."

"Great," he said. "I'll be there in twenty." He slid his phone back into his pocket and looked at his friends. "This could end in total disaster," he said grimly.

Eli nodded. "It could."

Gunner agreed, "A definite chance."

"It's a chance I gotta take," he finally said.

Without another thought, Jaxon ran to his truck and drove downtown as fast as he could without earning himself a speeding ticket that would eat up more of his time.

The main street was busy. Tourists standing in the middle of the road, taking photos of the two-lane street with the mountains in the back. He honked at the those in his way, until he found a parking spot and parked quickly.

It was only four thirty in the afternoon when he jogged toward the bar, and when he entered the bar was empty, which came as a relief. He didn't want anyone eavesdropping on his conversation. He walked in but stopped short when he saw the expression on Willow's and Aubrey's faces—they weren't livid with anger, but instead filled with sadness.

"What happened?" he asked, closing the distance quickly.

Willow and Aubrey traded a long glance before Aubrey gave Willow a nod to explain. She turned to him and said, "Charly's ex-fiancé, Marcel, got into a bad car accident last night. He was hit by a drunk driver then a big rig."

Jaxon took that in and didn't even know what to do with it. His first instinct was to say, *Why would she care?* The man betrayed her in the worst way possible. But he knew Charly and knew her heart was too big to totally turn her back on her ex.

Besides, Jaxon could tell by their expressions that it wasn't good, even without them having to explain further. "Is it serious?" he asked, folding his arms over his chest.

Aubrey nodded solemnly. "Very serious. He's on life support at the Arizona General Hospital and won't survive this."

Charly filled his mind, as did the confusion she must feel. Suddenly, the only thing he needed was to get her in his arms. He glanced around the bar. "Where is she?" He looked back at the two women. "Where is Charly?"

Willow's eyes softened. "She flew out to Phoenix a little while ago to be with him."

The emotions that suddenly hit Jaxon were practically blinding. Jealously, fury, desperation— it all flowed over him, and he felt selfish for even recognizing them in such a situation. Of course, she would have wanted to be there with Marcel, where else would she have gone? She had loved him once, after all, and not that long ago. That love would still remain, no matter that her heart had been shattered.

Aubrey finally broke the silence with a firm voice. "Why

did you come here, Jaxon? What did you want to talk about?"

He pushed away thoughts of himself and said, "I need you to help me make things right between Charly and me. What do I do? Do I beg her to give me another chance? Do I grovel?" He realized as he spoke, how could that happen now? Charly was about to lose someone she had shared deep love with, and planned to spend forever with. She'd been torn up before about not wanting to get into another relationship—now it would only be worse.

Willow and Aubrey exchanged another glance before Aubrey motioned for Jaxon to take a seat at one of the barstools.

"You're right, we do need to talk, and we can help you," Aubrey said, deep serious. "This must stay between us. If Charly even suspected we were talking about this, she'd go ballistic."

"Let's hear it then," he said, nodding her on, sliding onto the barstool.

Aubrey leaned back against the bar fridge, crossing her arms. "Charly cares about you, but she's too scared because somehow, she thinks what Marcel did to her was her fault. Like if she'd only been more aware she would have known the true person he was. She doesn't trust her judgement when it comes to her heart after all that happened with him. Especially considering how fast this all has happened. She was not expecting you—that much I know. And personally, I think all along she's been waiting for you to make a mistake so she could kind of tell herself: 'I told you so. You shouldn't trust yourself. You make bad judgements that will lead to disaster.' So, when she learned about your visit to Billy, she pounced on it, almost so it would blow her up first before you could get any closer."

Willow nodded in agreement. "You've managed to bring a lot of joy into her life since you met her. All the sparkle and liveliness she had before was gone. You saw her when you first came into the bar that first night, she was cold, withdrawn. But now when she's with you...we can see it all coming back. She's laughing again, loving life and enjoying herself. It's why she's struggling so much with her emotions. She wants to be happy, but everything is just messy, you know."

He nodded. "Yeah, I know." Because he'd done that to her. He'd given her a reason to doubt him.

Before he could say more, Aubrey said, "We like you for Charly."

Jaxon smiled for the first time since Charly left him, and asked, "While I appreciate that, does Charly like me for her?"

Willow nodded. "I know she does. She's just scared things with you are too good, too soon, and with everything with what you said to Billy, she was shaken." She paused, twining her finger around her braid tucked over her shoulder. "But I know she understands where you were coming from. I can guarantee that in the beginning she had ulterior motives for getting closer to you too."

"To use my relationship with the locals to her benefit," he offered.

Aubrey smiled and nodded. "Probably to outsmart you too. She wanted to win the game you two were playing."

Jaxon chuckled. "And damn, did she win." She won all of him. He couldn't even think straight.

Was this love? Where a man simply unraveled completely?

Taking in everything he'd heard, he bit his lip and looked down at his fingers tapping against the bar top before turning back to the two women who knew Charly best. "So how do I fix this? What should I do?"

"Don't disappoint her," Aubrey said.

Jaxon stared at Charly's friends, letting all their advice sink in slowly. He repeated the phrase silently over and over in his mind until finally, through their help, he had an epiphany. He suddenly knew exactly what he needed to do next.

He rose from the barstool and strode toward the entrance.

"Where are you going?" Willow asked him.

"I'm going to do what I said I was going to do," he called back over his shoulder. "I'm going to fix this." He took out his phone and dialed Gunner's number on his way toward the door.

"Do I need to come and save you?" Gunner asked, by way of answering the phone.

Jaxon said, more serious than he'd ever been in his life, "I need you to get ahold of that pilot friend of yours and organize a plane for me to Phoenix." Gunner had used this local private pilot on many occasions when he toured.

Gunner hesitated. Then asked, "Are you all right?"

He walked out of the bar and gave a reply without looking back, "I will be when I land in Phoenix."

Twenty-One

Charly sat next to the bed in the dimly lit hospital room as the constant beeping of monitors filled the air, a grim rhythm that reminded her of the situation. Wires and tubes snaked around, linking Marcel to the machinery that struggled to keep him alive. At the center of the bed, he lay frail—his skin pale and hollow—as if life was slowly slipping away from him. His face was almost unrecognizable with its bandages and bruises. She reached out and took his hand, yet she hadn't said a word since arriving. He felt warm but lifeless. She had simply stared at him, taking in a body that was no longer distinguishable from what it once was.

After calling his sister to tell her the news, who said she would get in touch with his family, Charly spent all afternoon with him, hoping for some sign that this was all a nightmare, an illusion of some kind that he would wake up from.

But that never happened.

There was no hope here, only death.

And as realization settled in, she exhaled sharply—a breath she felt like she had been holding ever since finding him with another woman.

"I didn't want it to end like this," she told him softly. "I wanted us to grow old together, have children who found love themselves. I wanted to look back on our lives without any regrets."

As if expecting an answer, she glanced at his face and waited for something—anything—that would show he could still hear her.

But there was nothing.

"When I found out about your cheating, I wanted you to really feel what it was like to be betrayed," she said, lacing her fingers in with his. "I wanted you to experience the pain and anguish that I went through when my world caved in around me." A tear escaped from her eye, but she didn't bother wiping it away. "I ignored all your attempts to reach me because I was so mad. I only hoped that you would hurt as much as I did, but I never wanted this to happen."

Her chest tightened and a lump clogged her throat. "You gave up on us," she said, her voice breaking, "and I'll never understand why."

Once more, she paused. Even with all that had occurred, she had never wished this upon him and regretted not telling him that she forgave him to lessen his shame. She was sure that she had more time to forgive him, more time to understand his actions, more time for...*something*.

As people spoke in hushed tones outside the door, faint

beams of sunlight peeked through half-closed blinds, adding a subtle glow to the white walls of the room. Her heart felt like it was breaking into a thousand pieces, shattering in this very moment. "I should have told you that life is too short to not be at your happiest. That I'll never forget the happy memories we had because those are there too. And now we'll never have that chance…"

She paused, waiting for any sign of recognition in his expression, a twitch of his lips or movement behind his eyelids.

Tears began streaming from her eyes despite herself, as all the rage she had felt toward him faded away and only sorrow remained.

He would never hear these words.

Regardless, she rose on shaky legs and leaned over, careful of all the wires, pressing her lips to his forehead. "I forgive you, Marcel, and I'm sorry I never got to tell you that to your face." She cupped the side of his face, adding, "In fact, I'm happy in Timber Falls. Maybe even happier than I've ever been. I'm there with Willow and Aubrey, and it's so peaceful and beautiful. You'd hate it—it's way too quiet, but I've realized I love it, and maybe I should have been there all long."

Her tears dripped onto his cheek. She brushed them away gently. "I don't regret the life I had with you. The good far outweighs the bad, and I'll never forget all the great times we had. When you go, I want you to leave in peace, knowing that I'm okay. In fact, more than all right, I'm happy." She pressed one last kiss to his cheek and then leaned away, right as her cell phone beeped with a call.

Sitting back in the chair, she grabbed her cell from her

purse and saw "Mom" on the caller ID. She wiped the tears from her face and inhaled sharply before answering into the receiver, "Mom."

"Charly, honey, are you okay?" Her mother's voice softened the heavy air. "I've just heard the news from Willow. Do you need us to come there?"

"I'm all right," she forced out. "Marcel isn't."

"I am so sorry," she said, and Charly had never heard her mother's voice sound so gentle. "This must be really confusing for you."

"Big-time." Though at the same time, a quiet she hadn't felt since she walked in on Marcel and Hannah at the bar. An image that she realized was slowly fading from her mind. When it first happened, she saw everything: their lustful expressions, exactly where Marcel's hands were and where Hannah's slid across his body. Now…those little details were fading. All she could see with him lying there was that she once loved him. "It's horrible. I feel so bad for June and Ron—" his parents "—and Mia."

"I do, too," her mom replied gravely. Whenever her parents came to visit Phoenix, they had many dinners with Marcel's parents. "Your father and I can jump on a plane and be there with you right away, if that would help. Do you need us?"

"No, it's okay," she said. The last thing she wanted was to be coddled by her mother. She'd mean well, but Charly needed time to process. "There's nothing you can do here anyway. I just…" She glanced at Marcel and felt the heat rising within her. "I just feel so guilty. I wished all kinds of horrible things upon him and now he's here—"

"Darling," her mother interjected softly. "You don't have the power to make bad things happen to anyone. This was an accident, caused by a drunk driver. Don't take that guilt onto yourself."

"I can't help it," she whispered.

Her mother didn't respond for a few seconds, then her father came on the line. "Charly, love?"

"Hi, Dad," she choked out.

"We're coming to you," he announced firmly. "I'm booking flights now. We'll be there just as soon as we can."

"Dad...you don't—" she began weakly, but he cut her off.

"We are coming," he repeated, leaving no room for argument.

Charly shut her eyes, feeling relief at his insistence. She needed her people around her, regardless if they fussed over her.

"Charly."

She snapped open her eyes and peered toward the door. Her heart sank when she saw Marcel's sister, Mia. She was five years younger than Marcel, but had his dark brown hair, dark eyes and olive complexion. Her red-rimmed eyes and blotchy skin showed that she had cried the entire flight there. Now her gaze fixed on her brother in the hospital bed—every ounce of color drained from her face as she surveyed him with horror.

"Dad," Charly began, "Mia is here. I must go."

"Of course," came his reply, "we'll see you soon. Love you."

"Love you, bye," Charly said, ending the call.

"I..." Mia's breath hitched and then she burst out sobbing. Charly was on her feet in a second, embracing Mia tightly. Even though she trembled and sobbed, the room was silent apart from them as they clung together until Charly gently parted away when Mia regained her composure.

Charly took Mia's hand. "Have you called your parents?" she asked.

"Yes," Mia said with a slow nod, "but they're on a cruise and won't be back in the port in Greece until tomorrow."

"You don't have to be alone," Charly reassured her, as something close to panic overtook Mia's expression, "I'll stay here with you."

Mia nodded gratefully, stepping away to stand beside her brother's bed, looking uncertain where to even touch him. "What did the doctor say?" she asked Charly softly, without glancing back at her.

"That she wanted to talk to the family," was Charly's careful response.

The look on the doctor's face when Charly first arrived at the hospital told her all she needed to know—the machine was keeping Marcel alive. The moment they turned it off, he would die.

"I understand," Mia stated, her voice trembling. She sat down on the bed near his legs. A long, heavy sighed passed through her lips. "I know he regretted hurting you. He probably would have carried that guilt for the rest of his life." Her voice faltered before she continued, "Though, he didn't deserve this."

"Of course, he didn't," Charly agreed helplessly. "Marcel made a bad judgement, but that doesn't make him a terrible person."

Glancing over her shoulder, Mia asked, "Do you for-give him?"

"I do," Charly said, giving a smile that felt honest and real through the tears. "Our paths ended, and that's okay. We had many wonderful memories together. I won't forget them."

Mia's breath hitched and tears flooded her cheeks.

Charly knew why—Marcel hadn't only hurt Charly, he had hurt his entire family who had grown to love Charly as part of their family.

Before Charly could say more, helping Mia find the same peace Charly had found, a cry of anguish echoed as the door squeaked open.

Charly couldn't move, shocked to see one of the last peo-ple she ever expected.

Mia immediately leaped up and threw herself at Hannah tightly. In that moment, Charly realized that Hannah had not just been a fling to Marcel.

Hannah wailed loudly, moving closer to Marcel on the bed as tears coursed down her face.

Charly couldn't look anymore, the pain pouring from Hannah was unbearable to witness. Instead, she shut her eyes against the overpowering sadness radiating from both women. Her heart felt like it had shattered into a million pieces, yet a truth hit her she could not ignore: she did not belong there anymore.

Forcing herself, she approached Mia, embracing her tightly in comfort. "I'm so sorry this happened to him," she murmured quietly. She glanced at Hannah, the woman whom Charly once wanted to wish horrible things upon, only to find Hannah staring back with red-ringed eyes full of despair. "It is so unfair." Glancing at Mia again, she added, "If you need me, call me."

"Thank you," said Mia, and Charly hugged her one last time.

She gave Hannah one final look as she wept, lying across Marcel's chest. The same woman who had been involved in ruining Charly's life, but only compassion overwhelmed Charly now. No one deserves this kind of pain.

Before she made it out the door, Hannah said, "Thank you, Charly. Thank you for being here for him."

Charly felt a warm comfort slide through her as she glanced over her shoulder. She had made peace with Marcel, and now she felt it was time to make peace with Hannah too. "I'm sorry that you've lost him," she said, before turning away and heading out the door.

Though as soon as she stepped out into the hallway, she stopped in her tracks.

As strong and confident as always, Jaxon strode straight for her, and in four large strides, he had her in his arms and embraced her tightly. She could feel the warmth radiating from him, and she melted into his hold, her voice breaking. "Jaxon…"

He planted a gentle kiss on her cheek, before wrapping his arm around her waist, holding her close. "Let's get you out of here."

She nodded, feeling a part of her broken heart begin to mend with every step she took down the hallway.

Twenty-Two

Just before entering the hotel near the hospital after landing in Phoenix, Charly gently pulled on his hand. He glanced to her as she asked, "Can we take a walk? I just need to clear my head before trying to sleep."

"Of course," he said.

She started walking in the opposite direction from the hotel. He followed, stepping into stride with her. They crossed the street and entered a small city park with lighted pathways and trees of all kinds. There were benches next to sturdy oak trees, which he guessed had been there for years judging by their massive canopies. They passed a sign that read Welcome to Margaret T. Hance Park. Established 1991.

"Did you come here a lot when you lived here?" he asked as they strolled along the wide paved path.

She nodded. "This park is named after the city's first female mayor. I always felt…strong when I came here. It helped me see past the little stuff I was going through to show me that with hard work anything is possible."

He glanced sidelong at her again and gave a small smile. "That sounds like something you would appreciate."

"Margaret Hance was an incredible woman," she said softly. "She most certainly inspired me."

An elderly couple strode by hand in hand, and Jaxon's chest warmed. He wondered if he would have even noticed them before he'd met Charly. She made him look at people in love in a whole new light—and with envy.

"I'm so sorry this has happened to Marcel," he said to her, uncertain these were the right words. "All of this must be very confusing."

"I'm sorry too," she said. She stopped walking and then turned to him. "And yes, it's confusing, because I wanted this for him."

Jaxon gathered her in his arms. "What do you mean?"

"I wished for the worst possible things to happen to him after he was unfaithful to me," she said, her voice hitching with emotion. "I caused this." At these words her tears began to fall.

He pulled her closer, leaving no space between them, feeling her trembling in his arms. "You didn't do this, Charly. You don't have that kind of power." He didn't let go until her shaking stopped before he pulled back enough to look into her watery eyes. "Don't take on his wrongdoings as yours. It's not your burden to carry. What you feel is because of his actions, and none of it would have been felt if he hadn't cheated—that is the only truth here."

"The girls said the same thing to me," she offered. "But… all this just feels…"

"Hard to understand," he offered.

"Yeah," she said, leaning her head against his shoulder. "Exactly, because yes, there was heartbreak, but there were also happy times."

He smiled, brushing his thumbs across her cheeks, taking moisture with them. "Keep those good memories close."

"But the bad happened too," she whispered.

"Make peace with those," he said. Not knowing if she needed this or not, he drew her close, hugging her tight. "It's okay that you loved him. It's okay that you hate him. It's okay that you'll miss him." He pressed a kiss to her forehead. "All of it, Charly, is okay."

She was silent a moment. He thought maybe he'd said something wrong, but then she clung to him and cried, her body trembling against him.

He dropped his head into her neck and held on, well acquainted with loss, and knowing sometimes the best thing to do was say nothing at all.

When her crying quieted, she wiped her face and began walking again.

The rest of the walk around the large pond was met in silence. Jaxon let her be with her thoughts, but he kept his arm around her, knowing he'd never let go.

As soon as he and Charly returned to the room, he found

his bag had been brought in, and he set Charly's bag next to his. One look at her and she seemed exhausted—like her spirit had been completely drained. "Come on," he said, taking her hand, leading her into the bathroom.

She followed silently and watched as he turned on the faucet, running her bath. Before heading out the door, he gave her hand a squeeze. "Relax. You need it."

"Thanks," she whispered, shutting the door behind him.

He headed for the menu on the nightstand and took a quick look, before picking up the phone. When room service answered the call, he said, "Can I get a charcuterie board and a bottle of your best whiskey with two glasses and ice."

"Yes, sir," the man with the gravelly voice said. "We'll get it up to you just as soon as we can."

Knocking off things he had to do before she got out of the tub, he grabbed his cell phone from his pocket and sent Willow and Aubrey a text in a group chat: I've taken Charly to a hotel here in Phoenix.

Willow instantly replied: Please give Charly our love, tell her we're here when she needs us.

Aubrey's text came a moment later: Ask her to call us when she has a minute. We can't stop thinking about her.

He texted back: I will. Good night. He followed up with a text in his group chat with Eli and Gunner: All is well. We're at the hotel now.

Both gave him a thumbs-up emoji, which was the male equivalent of what Willow and Aubrey had said.

With a sigh, he muted his phone and dropped the cell on the bedside table, right as there was a knock on the door. He opened it and the server strode in, placing the tray on the footstool at the end of the bed. After Jaxon tipped him, he left the room, shutting the door behind him.

Jaxon filled the glasses with ice and whiskey, and it occurred to him that he'd never done anything like this before with any woman. She made him think beyond his own needs. He wasn't there for himself. He was there for her, and he was damn sure he'd turn the world upside down if it meant she didn't have to feel any more pain. Because the warmth that touched his chest when he was with her filled an emptiness that he'd been running from for a long time. But being there now, communicating with Charly's friends like one of her family members, only made him surer that this was exactly where he was meant to be.

The bathroom door creaked open, and Charly stepped out with a white bathrobe wrapped around her. She was makeup-free, and her hair was still damp from the bath, and she'd never looked more beautiful.

He handed her one of the glasses of whiskey he had poured. "Thought you could use this," he said.

"I really could, thank you." She took the glass and sipped from it, settling down on the bed.

"Do you want something to eat?" he asked, gesturing to the charcuterie board.

She shook her head, gazing at her crossed legs. "No, not right now, but thank you."

The exhaustion that was evident in her expression made him feel helpless. "I sent a message to Willow and Aubrey," he said softly. "They're worried about you and would like to hear from you when you're feeling ready."

She finished her sip of whiskey, cringing at the burn likely rushing down her throat. "Okay, I'll call them soon. I just need…" She looked up at him, staring blankly. "I don't even know what I need, if I'm being honest."

"I think that's to be expected." He downed a big swig of the whiskey, before joining her on the bed. He wished he had some words that would make her feel better but didn't know where to begin.

"You came," she noted, ending the silence between them.

He looked over at her with a small nod. "I came."

"Why?" she asked, her brows drawn together.

"The thought of you being here alone ate me up. I didn't want you going through this by yourself, especially when it's your ex-fiancé in that hospital bed." He placed his hand on her thigh, her bare skin feeling warm from the hot water. "Are you doing okay?"

She let out a deep sigh and then stared into her glass for a moment before setting it down on the nightstand beside her. Turning toward him, she adjusted her robe over her legs and sat cross-legged while facing him.

For a long minute, she examined him with a quizzical look in her eyes.

"Are you waiting for me to say something?" he asked with caution.

Her lips pursed for a moment before she blurted out, "I care about you and I don't want to push you away."

He knew he heard those words correctly but couldn't believe what he was hearing. "Say that again?"

"I care about you, and I don't want to push you away," she repeated, confidently. She chuckled lightly at whatever was showing on his expression and shook her head. "You might think I'm a bit out of my mind, but when I was with Marcel, all I could think about was that I wished I told him that I forgave him. I wish I told him how happy I am in Timber Falls. How happy I've been with you and this new life I built. I don't want to push away the chance of the happiness I always wanted, just because that happiness didn't happen with someone else. I want to stay open to falling in love again."

He finally processed what she had said and blinked. "You care about me and don't want to push me away?" The last conversation they had she was walking away from him. His brain had trouble catching up with this switch.

She gave a little shrug, smiling sweetly. "I know that this is probably confusing because of how we left things, but there it is, I have feelings for you. And I don't want to spend another minute not expressing what's in my heart. After being with Marcel today, I realized that we only get one life to live. That's it. Then it's over. And I refuse to make the same mistake again by not expressing how I feel because it scares me to do so. I want to be happy, and I want

to let love grow where it grows, and right now, it's growing with you."

Rational thought began to disappear from his conscious
mind. She squealed with delight as he brought her close and
held her tightly beneath him.

"Everything you've said is the best damn thing I've ever
heard," he murmured before leaning down and planting a
kiss on her lips, silencing any response she may have been
trying to give before he declared, "Because I never want
to let you go." There, he threw out the statement and let it
seep in the air between them.

He moaned when his mouth met hers and she fell into
the truth hanging between them. He craved to feel her and
needed to taste her, so he started a trail of kisses along her
jawline and down to her neck, where he teased and bit her
skin. He didn't stop until his mouth had found its way to
her chest where he opened the robe, uncovering two rosy,
taut nipples. He licked one, then sucked the other, taking
her breasts in his grasp, before continuing down even farther. His shoulders ended up between her legs as he licked
along one inner thigh and she quivered in response.

"Am I where you want me, Kitten?" he asked as he blew
softly across her heated, wet skin.

"Yes," she breathed out with a raspy voice, arching up
off the bed in answer.

Needing her just as much, he didn't hesitate any longer.
He licked over her sensitive flesh, until he reached her clit,
and focused his attention there. He flicked, swirled and

nipped the little bud, faster and harder each time until she was grinding against him, moaning as she threaded her hands into his hair, holding him to her.

When she hung, dangling on the edge of pleasure, he inserted two fingers into her slick sex and moved them in sync with his tongue until she was riding his hand and trembling beneath his mouth.

Not a minute later, she screamed out loud when the pleasure took over completely, claiming the climax until it consumed her entirely.

While she came down from the high, breathlessly a beautiful mess, he gave a final lick taking some of her sweet arousal with him, tasting all of her for himself.

She tilted up her chin, and he gazed into her hooded eyes with a grin. Then he found himself on his knees, her sweet, warm body pressed against him. She gave him a passionate kiss, while frantically unbuttoning his clothing until he was completely nude. Her lips trailed down to his chest as she paused to give him a playful smirk.

"You're going to kill me with those grins," he groaned, but she only laughed in response.

Taking his rock-hard cock in hand, she spoke softly, "Can't kill you just yet. I still have some use for you."

He chuckled, brushing his knuckles across her pinkish cheek, not expecting the pleasure that followed when she pulled his cock further into her mouth. She began to swirl her tongue around his shaft and the tip, seeming to savor every moment. The sensations left him unable to do anything apart from moaning in pleasure.

As if determined to make him blow, her movements quickly intensified, from the way she sucked to how fast she moved her hand; he threw his head back and grunted.

Until, the pleasure, her beauty, it all became too much. Wanting to finish wrapped within her, he gathered her in his arms and tossed her onto the bed beneath him. "I need you," he growled.

He didn't need to ask her twice. She spread her legs and he saw her sex glistening with arousal. Swearing under his breath, he quickly put on a condom and pulled her closer to him by the ankle. She laughed when their skin touched, but the sound was cut off as he guided his cock toward her drenched heat.

Their moans joined as one as he thrust into her in one swift movement, burying himself in her heat. "Damn, Kitten, what you do to me," he groaned against her neck before lifting her leg higher over his arm. He stayed still for a moment, savoring the feeling of being connected to her before he increased the pace of his thrusts.

Charly's mouth opened wider with pleasure, followed by a gasp each time he moved within her and another when he slowly withdrew, inch by inch. She reached up to caress his face, pulling back to look at him. He wanted to take in every moment—not miss a damn thing. He craved to see every sensation flicker across her face as she unraveled in his arms. He moved his hips faster, and harder, building the pleasure higher and higher, as skin slapped against skin and the musky scent of their sex filled the air.

Until her soaking wet heat clamped against him tight, and she began losing control, bucking against him, screaming out his name with pleasure.

Even then, he couldn't take his eyes away. He didn't want to miss a second of this, when she felt like something he had never felt before.

She felt like…*his*.

He grunted against her climax rolling in waves over his shaft and waited for her gaze to meet his as he moved within her again. Harder. Faster. He didn't stop.

When her eyes reopened and connected with his, he felt himself ready to come apart at the same time she reached a new peak of satisfaction. In that moment, he let go and unleashed all the desire within him.

As she tightened around him, he gave her every drop of himself, thrusting forward, roaring his relief, spilling inside her.

Many, *many* minutes later, when they regained their senses, her legs were tangled in his, and they lay breathless, a mess of satisfaction in each other's arms.

An easy silence settled in for a long while until she broke it by saying, "I'm going to have to say here in Phoenix for a few days until the funeral. I don't want to miss it, and there is no sense in traveling all the way home just to come back."

Damn, did he like hearing her call Timber Falls *home*.

He pulled her closer and kissed the top of her head. "I'll stay with you."

She leaned away, looking properly satisfied to her bones. "Are you sure? You really want to attend my ex-fiancé's funeral?"

He inclined his head without hesitation. "I'll be there, for you...with you." For all the paths he'd taken in his life, he felt this one was finally right. One that would bring him closer to what his parents had and what they stood for. One that would bring him happiness.

She watched him closely before hitting him with a grin. "Romantic. Sweet. Hot as hell. A devil in the bedroom." The heat faded from her eyes replaced by a warmth that filled Jaxon up, as she added, "You know, cowboy, you might just be pretty damn perfect."

"I'm only perfect, because of *you*," he said, tucking her hair behind her year. "To be what you deserve." And as he slid his mouth across hers, he vowed to make sure she never forgot that.

Jaxon and it was glaringly obvious he won them over. Jaxon talked sports with her father, and everything else with her mother, bringing her flowers or wine to any visit they had.

In the midst of it all, Jaxon got a glimpse into Charly's former life in Phoenix. Her old house and her old bar. Every little corner that she had visited told its own story of her past life. Somehow sharing this all with him felt like the closure she needed to leave Phoenix forever and never look back.

As her father shook Jaxon's hand, her mother asked her, "Are you ready for this?"

Charly nodded. "Yes, I'm ready to say goodbye." To Marcel. To Phoenix. To her old life.

Her mom gave her a reassuring smile, squeezed Charly's hand tight, and then stepped away as her father embraced Charly before heading toward the church.

Charly blew out slowly as Jaxon slipped his fingers through hers, holding her hand tight, as they followed in behind her parents moving up the church's steps. The choir, positioned in the loft above, sang beautifully into the air.

The church was breathtaking. The walls were built with durable stone. Sunlight poured in through stained glass windows, casting an array of colors that sparkled off the polished wood benches and marble flooring. Flickering candles surrounded the front, offering a soft glow, reminding Charly light could always be found in darkness.

She squeezed Jaxon's hand as she caught sight of the urn containing Marcel's ashes at the front of the church, adorned with floral arrangements. He held her hand as firm as ever,

Twenty-Three

Three days later, after spending all those days in Phoenix with Jaxon at her side, Charly approached the small white church set back from the road. Dressed in a little black dress that she'd picked up from a shop downtown, she glanced next to her at Jaxon, and smiled. He wore a proper black suit with a white dress shirt and black tie. He looked...*striking*. Fancy looked good on him.

"Charly," her mother called. "Jaxon."

She turned, catching her mom and dad approaching from the parking lot, both dressed in black attire.

When her mother reached her, she took Charly into a warm hug, and then offered the same affection to Jaxon. While the past days were filled with sadness, as they went over to Marcel's parents' house to comfort them after they had taken Marcel off life support, and he passed away, the days were also full of life. Her parents had gotten to know and they took their seats behind Marcel's parents and Mia, where they'd asked them to sit. Hannah sat next to Mia, her head down, her shoulders shaking with her quiet sobs.

Charly breathed in deeply and out just as slow, shutting her eyes. The sadness surrounded her was near suffocating, but she held on to Jaxon's hand, her anchor in this storm.

She opened her eyes as the clergyman, draped in flowing robes, came forward after all the mourners took their seats. He stood at the podium. His voice steady and gentle filled the room as he welcomed Marcel's family and friends to the service.

Marcel's loved ones began stepping forward, offering eulogies and sharing memories, their voices filled with both sadness and joy. The last person to speak was Hannah, and she spoke of her love with Marcel and the profound impact Marcel had on her life. Charly could feel the gazes burning into the back of her head, but this moment belonged to Hannah, not her. She no longer had Marcel's heart.

With Jaxon's hand holding hers, Charly only felt sadness for Hannah that this love she shared with Marcel was now gone.

When Hannah returned to the pew, the clergyman stepped forward to the podium again, and said, "Though our hearts are heavy with grief, let us take comfort in the fond memories we have of Marcel—the laughter, stories and love that continue to live within us. As we pay final tribute, it is important to recognize that even though Marcel's physical body may no longer be here, Marcel's spirit will never die. The memory of Marcel should bring us solace and motivation to live our lives to the fullest."

...*and motivation to live our lives to the fullest*, had stayed with Charly for the remainder of the service, echoing in her ears.

As the family, and Hannah, left the church, she followed Jaxon out behind her parents and headed outside to where the family waited to greet the crowd.

Jaxon went ahead of her, saying gently to Marcel's mother, "I'm deeply sorry for your loss," before he moved on to his father.

Charly stepped in front of June, who always put on a strong face. She took Charly into her arms, but her trembling body revealed her unbearable pain. "Thank you for being here. It's more than anyone could have asked of you."

"I wanted to be here," Charly said, holding her as tight as she could muster. "I am so, so sorry."

"I am sorry too," June said. She kissed Charly's cheek. "Be happy, Charly. Marcel would want that for you."

"Thank you," Charly said, her voice shaking, but she refused to let any more tears fall. She turned to Ron and hugged him.

He said softly, "Be well, my dear."

"You as well," she said, squeezing him one last time. When she moved into Mia's arms, she said, "Don't be a stranger. You're always welcome to visit us in Timber Falls."

"I'll make sure to take a trip out soon," Mia said, leaning away with tears streaming down her face. "No matter what happened, you're always my friend."

"And you are mine," Charly said, squeezing Mia's arms.

As she let go of Mia, walking away from the family she thought would be part of every holiday, she caught sight of Jaxon and confidently walked away from her past to step happily into her bright future.

Her gaze fell to Hannah, being hugged by her friend. Charly offered a small smile of comfort before she walked away.

"We need to get to the airport," Jaxon said, twining his fingers with hers.

…and motivation to live our lives to the fullest, stayed on Charly's mind as she went to the airport with her parents. They parted ways in the terminals as they took their flight to Ann Arbor, and she and Jaxon took their flight home.

By the time she was seated on the plane, she felt those words said by the clergyman resonate inside her. She would do exactly what he said—she would *live*.

The flight home was exhausting, and by the time they arrived at the bar, she thought she should have gone home. But the moment she walked into the bar and was hit by a wave of noise and energy, she awakened. The bar felt electric, filled with laughter, chatter and life.

As the door shut behind them, Willow, who stood on stage, asked the crowd, "Tonight we are playing the Battle of the Sexes. Each game will be a series of skill-based challenges. Participants will compete in arm wrestling, darts, a dance-off and beer pong."

The crowd roared in approval, and Charly breathed in

the excitement in the air, needing this more than anything. Around her were women and men, some cowboys, some not, but everyone was happy and that filled all the cold spots in her soul from the funeral with heady warmth.

She moved toward the bar where Gunner and Eli were sitting on stools, with Aubrey behind the bar.

Aubrey caught sight of her and moved to her in an instant. "Thank goodness you're back," she breathed, throwing her arms around Charly tight. After being thoroughly squished to death by her hug, Charly felt right where she belonged. Aubrey glanced over Charly's face thoroughly before she said, "It's been a very long day for you. Are you sure you want to be here tonight?"

She nodded. "Honestly, this is exactly where I want to be right now." She needed love—and Willow and Aubrey were her people. The women who had seen her through all the good times and hard times in her life.

"Come sit down and I'll get you both some drinks. You both look like you need one," Aubrey said. The long embrace she gave Jaxon let her know that she'd forgiven him for his misgivings and he'd been accepted into their little family.

Gunner rose. "I'm sorry to hear of your loss, Charly." He offered her a hug, as did Eli.

"Thanks," Charly said, taking a seat on the empty stool. "I appreciate it."

Aubrey poured two beers, and dropped them in front

of them before making her way to a customer at the end of the bar.

Charly grabbed her beer and chugged it, attempting to ease the weariness of the day, as Jaxon pulled up a stool next to her. He tugged her in between his legs as they watched the game go on amidst laughter in the crowd.

It wasn't until Jaxon hugged her from behind that she realized the game had ended with the ladies declared the winners, while she'd been drinking her beer absentmindedly. Gunner's melodic voice suddenly filled the room, the crowd now filling up the dance floor. Exhaustion suddenly sank into her, reminding her she probably should have gone home.

"You're home."

She blinked into focus, finding a teary-eyed Willow in front of her. "I'm home." And it occurred to her that she felt more at home in Timber Falls than she'd ever felt in her life. "I missed you."

Willow gave her a warm smile, opening her arms. "I missed you too." She threw herself around Charly, holding on tight. "I wanted to be there with you."

"You couldn't have been. You had to be here," Charly said, pulling away from Willow's embrace. "Besides, you were there anyway. In here." She placed her hand over her heart. "Always in here."

"Don't you know it," Willow said. She kissed Charly's cheek then added, "I better go help Aubrey."

"Do you need my help?" Charly asked.

"Gosh, no, you go rest," Willow said firmly, leaving no room for argument. "Breakfast tomorrow at the Sparrow?"

Charly smiled, knowing she had a million questions she'd have to answer. "Always."

After Willow waved goodbye to Jaxon, he wrapped his arms around her again from behind, pulling her tight against his chest. "Ready to leave?" he asked.

The crowd cheered as the band began playing a slow song and Gunner's warm gravelly voice spread throughout the bar. Charly set down her empty bottle, stood up and clutched his hands. She wanted to end this night with a happy memory. "One dance first, then we'll go," she said with a smile.

"That we can do." He took her onto the dance floor and they swayed together under the dim lights.

She rested her head against his chest with one of his hands resting on her back, the other lower on her bottom. The air was infused with his woodsy scent and she melted into him.

Until he tucked a finger under her chin and then she met emotion-packed eyes. She'd seen Jaxon be many things before—many sexy, *sexy* things—but nothing compared to him now. His gaze seemed determined and decided as he stepped closer to her.

Her breath caught in her throat when he smiled warmly at her, and the crowd slowly faded from around her.

"What is it?" she asked.

His voice was steady…*strong*, as he put his focus wholly on her. "I fought against giving up this bar, the last piece of myself, and to fall into my father's role. But I know now this bar is in the right hands. Your beautiful hands." Taking her by the waist, he brought her a little bit closer. "I'm the first one to admit I never believed in the magic in the mountains or the legend." He slowly shook his head, his eyes bright, focusing intently on her. "What a fool I've been."

She smirked at him. "You won't hear me arguing with you on that point."

He cracked a smile and gave her another wink. "I thought you might agree." He stopped dancing and cupped her face. "I realized on that plane to Phoenix that I don't want to go through another day with the world not knowing that we're together."

Pressing herself against him, she smiled. "I wouldn't be opposed to that."

"Good." He stared at her with warmth and tenderness. "Because I like the idea of calling you my girlfriend."

She smiled in return "That does have a nice ring to it."

"Sure as hell does." His smile could have brought light to pure darkness and melted her heart as he gathered her in his arms. Placing her back on her feet, he kissed her with such passion that all thoughts of anything else disappeared.

Until Gunner's voice broke through the quiet moment between them, and she remembered they weren't alone. Though as she backed away, catching the warmth in Jaxon's gaze, she realized in that very second how all her heartbreak had led to this moment. Because now she knew how fragile life was, and in this life, she wanted this future…with Jaxon.

Epilogue

Two months had passed since Jaxon made things official between them. Two months of peaceful mornings with him at the ranch…and fun nights at the bar. Two months of sneaking off wherever possible for a quickie. Because somehow Charly could not keep her hands off him.

She attempted to catch her breath as Jaxon guided her away from the rear of the barn, her face still rosy after he pressed her up against the wall and proved he couldn't keep his hands off her either.

"Us sneaking off to have a quickie is becoming a habit," she said, as the quiet night surrounded them, crickets singing off in the distance.

Jaxon glanced over his shoulder and winked at her. "A wonderful habit that we should continue for years to come."

She laughed, all the while secretly hoping nobody had seen them leave the campfire. In the distance, she could hear Gunner's voice and Decker's guitar were playing together in harmony.

All the cowboys and Aubrey and Willow had helped Charly move in with Jaxon today, then they rounded out the evening with pizza and a fire. Jaxon had posed the question of moving in only a week ago. Now living with her heart leading the way, she had accepted. She wanted to wake up next to Jaxon and go to sleep in his arms.

Through the move she'd experienced a range of emotions—happy to be moving in with Jaxon yet sad to not stay living with Willow and Aubrey. Twenty minutes ago, she'd been in tears with her girlfriends. Now she was a panting mess of satisfaction.

Life was weird. Perhaps it was time for her to ease up on the drinks for a bit.

Jaxon firmly held her hand as they stepped around the corner of the barn, but then he froze in his tracks. She stumbled right into him. "Ouch!" she complained.

"Shhh," he whispered, raising a finger to his lips. "Look."

She quietly peered around the corner and stared in astonishment at the scene before them. Willow and Eli were almost tearing one another's clothes off, their kisses hot and passionate, and not something she and Jaxon should watch.

She threw her hands over her eyes immediately, backing away. "What do we do?" she whispered.

"This is the only way to get back to the fire," he answered, just as quietly. "Do we really want to stick around here and hear what happens next between them?"

"No," Charly said, shoving him forward.

Jaxon chuckled. Then he coughed noisily to get their attention. "Sorry to intrude," he called, "but this is the only route back to the fire."

Willow gasped, and Charly looked just in time to see her pushing Eli away—hard.

Caught off guard, Eli went soaring back, landing on his ass. "What the hell?" he groaned.

"Oh, no," Willow said, reaching out to help him before stopping herself. She glanced at Charly then Jaxon.

Charly bit her lip as Willow's face turned the deepest shade of red she'd ever seen.

"I'm so sorry," Willow eventually said.

Even Charly was struggling not to laugh now. She tugged on Jaxon's hand. "We'll just…um…meet you back at the fire," she said, hurrying away, hearing Jaxon in hysterics behind her.

Once they were far enough away, Charly let out a fit of laughter. "I had no idea that was going on," she said. "Did you?"

Jaxon pulled her close, wrapping his arm around her neck and kissing her head. "No idea, but they did look pretty cozy didn't they?"

"Definitely comfortable." She smiled.

Jaxon turned his gaze to hers. "Do you think it's a good thing that Eli and Willow might be getting together?" he asked curiously.

"I think so," she replied. "They've been through something very similar. I like Eli—he's made of good stuff, right?"

Jaxon nodded. "I'm probably biased because I've known him my whole life, but I don't think anyone would be better for Willow than Eli."

She smiled, leaning into him, as he wrapped his arms around her tight. "Maybe, but I'm not sure how he'll fare when it comes to Aubrey. She can be quite protective of Willow."

Jaxon pressed a quick, soft kiss to her mouth and grinned. "I'm sure Eli will manage fine."

"We shall see," Charly replied seriously. Aubrey was a force, and she wasn't sure Eli could stand against it.

They moved closer toward the fire, until Jaxon stopped near the house. In the distance, the cowboys, as well as some women Charly didn't know, were singing along with Gunner and Decker, accompanied by some very entertaining dance moves—no doubt the result of the empty beer bottles around them.

Jaxon tilted his head down at Charly. Emotion filling his eyes as he said, "I wish my parents could have seen this—seen you here. They would have loved you and loved you for me."

Warmth settled deep into her chest, and she rose, sliding her arms around his neck. "I wish I could have met them too. But we'll remember them as we make our own memories here."

"Maybe even our own family," he murmured in agreement.

She expected to feel anxious at his words, yet the worry never came. "Maybe so," she said gently. Then she added with a laugh, "In the future."

Jaxon hesitated. His eyes showing a hint of apprehension. "Boys," he said at last, his voice almost a whisper, "I should say I want boys. No girls."

She scoffed. "We are *not* starting this again. What is wrong with girls?"

He lowered his chin, meeting her at eye level and said with complete seriousness, "I can only handle one of you. A whole houseful could be my downfall."

She burst out laughing, unable to help herself. "I hate to break it to you, but there's something you should know about my family," she replied playfully as she strode away from him and toward their friends at the fire.

"What's that?" Jaxon called after her.

"We haven't had a boy in the family for three generations," she called over her shoulder, and laughed even harder as his curse echoed across the night sky.

★ ★ ★ ★ ★